Advance Praise

"Larry Brown once said, 'The best literature is always about matters of the human heart,' and that's precisely where Ellen Prentiss Campbell dares go in her new collection *Known by Heart*. These are mature tales that have earned their knowledge and resonance. Precise as open-heart surgery, laying bare the more rarely seen inner chambers of love's entropy and endurance, its old flames and addictions, even the ridiculous vanity of self-love. Ms. Prentiss Campbell's work pulses with pain and pleasure. Intricate, vulnerable, and above all, compassionate."

> — Marc Nieson, author of *Schoolhouse: Lessons on Love & Landscape*

"What stories we tell, whose stories are told, are crucial matters, and Ellen Prentiss Campbell takes great care in her choices and in their telling. *Known by Heart*, a beautifully detailed study of human intimacy—with all its loves and sorrows—unfolds in the voice of a gifted writer, who remembers to include the small unknown betrayals, the too-often-neglected human kindnesses, revealing the space between us, which she reminds us aches like a 'phantom limb.' These stories will hurt in their loss and offer solace in helping us remember we aren't 'quite done yet.'"

> —Todd Davis, author of *Native Species* and *Winterkill*

"Keen psychological insight and a poetic flair for language bring these stories to vivid life. Campbell's characters struggle to escape their dilemmas, whether the confines of stifling families or their own minds. To the reader's delight, some characters pop up in multiple stories, weaving a world of recognizable human longings that are credible, poignant, and beautifully described."

> — Donna Baier Stein, author of *Sympathetic People* and *Scenes from the Heartland*

"The stories in Ellen Prentiss Campbell's *Known by Heart* burst with lyricism and a depth of human understanding. This is a moving and beautifully written collection that tells us so much about the complex nature of love."

> — Elizabeth Poliner, author of *As Close to Us As Breathing* and *Mutual Life & Casualty*

"Ellen Prentiss Campbell prefaces her intense collection of short stories *Known by Heart* with a line from *The Riddle Song:* 'What is the story that has no end?' The answer is *love,* a complicated and ever-shifting answer… Campbell knows that old longings and lost loves continue long after the physical lovers disappear…and lovers most keep what they most lose—with paradoxical intensity."

> — Lois Marie Harrod, author of *Fragments from the Biography of Nemesis*

Known By Heart

Known By Heart

Collected Stories

Ellen Prentiss Campbell

Apprentice
House Press
Loyola University Maryland

First Edition

Casebound ISBN: 978-1-62720-262-6
Paperback ISBN: 978-1-62720-263-3
Ebook ISBN: 978-1-62720-264-0

Printed in the United States of America

Cover design by Chelsea McGuckin, featuring "Girl Writing" by Milton Avery, courtesy of The Phillips Collection, Washington, D.C.

Promotion plan developed by Jacqueline Kohaut

Published by Apprentice House Press

Apprentice
House Press
Loyola University Maryland

Apprentice House Press
Loyola University Maryland
4501 N. Charles Street
Baltimore, MD 21210
410.617.5265
www.ApprenticeHouse.com
info@ApprenticeHouse.com

For Harry, Rebecca, Tim and Martha,
As the riddle song says, the story of I love you has no end.

Also by Ellen Prentiss Campbell

Contents

Some stories in this collection first appeared in print as follows:

"Problem Set" in *The American Literary Review, Volume XXIV, Number 1*
"Your Guardian, Angela" in *The MacGuffin, Volume XXVIII, Number 3*
"A Long Time to Be Gone" in *Trachodon, Issue 4*
"Duets and Solos" in *Talking River, Issue 28*
"Faith and Practice" in *Backbone Mountain Review, 2010*
"Out of this World" in *Glossolalia, Volume 1:4*
"Known by Heart" in *Kaleidoscope, Number 59*
"Antiques and Collectables" in *REAL, Volume 32.1*
"Estates and Trust" in *Fourth River, Issue 2, Spring*
"Fugitive Day" in *Bryant Literary Review, Volume 8*
"Surprise Boxes" in *Spindrift, 2006*
"The Spring" in *Blueline, Volume XXVIII*

Problem Set

Joy navigated past a stream of trucks. She hated highway driving, mistrusted her night vision. Since turning fifty last year she battled what the ophthalmologist called floaters. In Breezewood, the trucks roared onto the Pennsylvania turnpike while she continued on Route 30 toward Bedford.

Bedford, midway between her home in D.C. and his in Pittsburgh, served as the usual rendezvous point. They ate the first dinner of their weekends in the Jean Bonnet, a stone tavern at the junction of what had been two trails and then two post roads, centuries before the turnpike. Friday night locals crowded the bar for darts and beer; Joy and Daniel preferred the dining room downstairs. The thick stone walls and heavy beams muffled the din of the juke box above.

Arriving first, Joy settled into their favorite table by the fireplace. The hearth's warmth relaxed her from the drive and the hectic week at school. A high school physics teacher, Joy had a briefcase full of problem sets to grade in the car. Now that she and Daniel met more often, she was falling behind in her work. Teaching required so much prep and clean up time. She should work until he came but, instead, Joy ordered a glass of red wine and the artichoke dip.

They had met four years before; stranded in an ice storm in the Atlanta airport, respective connections cancelled. During the delay, over tepid coffee in paper cups, he told her about his wife Selma.

Selma always had been healthy, except for one life-threatening episode of eclampsia fifteen years earlier at their daughter Monica's birth. The doctors warned against more children; she took up running and kept blood pressure, cholesterol, and weight low. Approaching forty, she trained for her first marathon—a challenge in celebration of the milestone birthday. Every morning Selma ran the steep hills of their neighborhood. One morning, cooling down from her run, she collapsed in the driveway: a massive cardiac event.

Unknowing, Daniel sat inside over breakfast, reading the paper until a neighbor pounded on the door. Daniel began CPR learnt years before to qualify as a chaperone for their daughter's scout trips. The paramedics arrived; Selma never regained consciousness. He blamed himself for not finding her sooner. He blamed himself for not taking up running fifteen years ago. He should have been with her.

The doctors suggested disconnecting life support. Daniel deferred, neither he nor Monica was ready to give up hope. Besides, he felt uncertain of Selma's wishes. To his surprise, she hadn't listed herself as an organ donor on her driver's license. They'd never executed advance directives: that sloppiness his fault, too. Dodging the bullet when Monica was born should have warned him.

Insurance for acute hospitalization ended. At this point in recounting the story in the airport, he crumpled the empty Starbucks cup in beautiful hands—large hands, with long fingers. He wore a wedding ring.

Sounding angry, Daniel continued. *I caved in and gave permission to pull the plug.*

He arrived for the last shift of vigil alone; prepared to lie to Monica, to say her mother had slipped away. But Selma—blessed or cursed by her runner's constitution—breathed on, on her own, neither waking nor dying. She had hovered in limbo for almost six months by the night Joy met Daniel.

Snow and ice socked in the airport; delays became cancellations. They rode the shuttle bus to the airport hotel and drank snifters of brandy in the bar; the Muzak system played a terrible canned version of *Norwegian Wood.* They boarded the elevator, each with a key card for a room. At her floor, she picked up his suitcase. "Come with me," she said, shocking herself. Forty-six years old, a confirmed solitary, Joy lived carefully by scientific method: recognizing a problem, collecting data,

2

testing her hypothesis. All experiments and evidence so far had proved relationships required more heat energy than she could spare. She considered herself deficient in some way, her own name an ironic misnomer.

In the dark anonymous room, lying beneath the synthetic beige blanket, they warmed the antiseptic sheets. She had almost forgotten, almost forsworn the genuine, reciprocal delight of using another body, and being used—passionately used, tenderly used.

The next morning she awoke disoriented in the suffocating artificial darkness. While Daniel spoke softly on the phone with his daughter, Joy showered—to give him privacy, and reclaim her own.

They embraced in the airport departures lounge. "I don't know when I can see you again, but I want to," he said. "It's not right, to drag you into my situation. I can't promise anything, offer anything."

"Don't worry," she said. "I'm quite self-sufficient. Famous for it, actually."

On the flight home she thought about him. She tried to dissect what had prompted her uncharacteristic boldness the night before. Instinct? Perhaps, but something more complicated than simple desire: a yearning to offer solace. Joy held the secret of him like a piece of gold in her pocket as she resumed routine.

He left a message while she was out the following Friday night, at the concert series she attended with a colleague.

"This is a singing telegram," he said and sang—not badly—all the verses of *Norwegian Wood*. He made her laugh and want to call him back.

She waited until morning and savored their first long conversation, curled in bed beneath her white duvet, luxuriating in her light-drenched room—with him and alone, at the same time.

Joy never considered it an affair. That implied deceit and hurt. She betrayed no one. Nor did he, by any reasonable standard, although Selma still slumbered in her netherworld and Daniel wore his ring.

"I'm sorry," he said. "It's not fair to you that I'm not free."

Joy wouldn't have respected him if he could easily shrug off his wife. She appreciated his loyalty to Selma, or rather to the idea of Selma, her memory.

And she suspected, from past experiments, she would not have wanted him if he had been free.

The space between them—temporal, geographic and emotional—suited Joy. By familiar paradox, she found it easier to be intimate when protected by distance. Separation fostered closeness as it had with her childhood pen pal. Free from the pressure of daily interactions, Joy had confided on the page. The other girl wrote her family was coming East to see Washington D.C. Joy's mother invited them to dinner. Meeting face-to-face, the pen pals turned shy. Afterward, the correspondence petered out.

Until recently, Daniel and Joy could meet only at occasional, irregular intervals. He visited Selma's nursing home bedside almost every day. And the more urgent problem requiring his vigilance was Monica's unsettled, extended adolescence: dangerous exploits with drugs, drinking, and sex. Daniel attributed the acting out to losing her mother and reproached himself.

Joy had never met the girl but suspected Monica might be wild by temperament, one of those incorrigibles who go off the rails even with both parents fully present. She thought Daniel could have practiced tougher love with Monica: pulled her out of public school, placed her in a school like her own Sacred Heart Academy. A lay teacher, not a Catholic herself, Joy held no illusions that a single-sex parochial school constituted safe haven. Plenty of her students found trouble, too, but at least it required more effort.

Last year, nineteen-year-old Monica dropped out of college and had a baby. One more disaster it seemed at first, but she proved a conscientious mother. She married the father, an electrician. Daniel liked him, as well as the union health benefits for his daughter and granddaughter.

And turning over the worry, he really liked that. And being able to see Joy twice a month: he left work early on alternate Fridays, dropped in at the nursing home, and headed out of town.

Joy found the more frequent reunions disconcerting. The new rhythm required adjustment. Fatigued, fragmented, she lacked her usual home weekend quota of quiet time alone. Her spacious, sparely furnished apartment looked untidy and neglected. Last night she'd almost called to cancel. But she neither wanted to lie nor tell him the truth. She could not disappoint him.

Now Daniel entered the tavern. Relieved, Joy observed her response to his physical presence: a rush of pleasure. Stop overthinking, she chided herself.

He kissed her and then slid into the seat across the table, brown eyes glowing. "You look beautiful."

The arrangement still worked, even with the shorter cycle of separation and reunions. Perhaps she would acclimate. Reassured, she fell into table talk and pleasant anticipation of the night to come.

After dinner she followed his red taillights along Route 30, the two-lane Lincoln Highway which still stretched all the way from New York to California. The darkness of country roads unnerved her. How had the first settlers walked west beneath endless tree cover? A pickup truck careened over the hill and shot past her too fast, its driver drunk or high. The thin pages of the local paper bore witness to plenty of desperation: hit and runs, driving under the influence, domestic abuse, bankruptcies.

Cresting the next hill, Daniel turned at the floodlit sign. *Lincoln Motor Courts.* Their headlights swept over half a dozen cottages, like playhouses or the Amish sheds for sale throughout the region. *Vacancy!* blinked pink neon cursive letters in the office window. A boxy Coke machine stood by the door.

Joy waited in her car, letting Daniel pick up the keys. She felt self-conscious arriving in two cars, uncomfortable at the prospect of scrutiny by whoever manned the desk in this out-of-the-way place. Two consenting adults owed no one any explanation, and no one cared, but she preferred to stay at bigger places like the restored resort hotel just outside of Bedford. However, Daniel insisted on paying for their lodging and Joy worried about cost, now they were seeing each other so often. At her suggestion, to economize, they were trying different places—without great success, so far. She had judged the bed and breakfast in town too cluttered with doilies, the small motel close to the lake bare and ugly, and the guest room upstairs from the bar at the Jean Bonnet noisy. These old-fashioned tourist cabins had been Daniel's idea; Joy was dubious. She missed room service and spa massages. She missed quiet luxurious rooms at the end of long anonymous corridors.

So far neither had invited the other home, nor broached the possibility. It would mean double travel time for whoever visited. Explanations and introductions would be required, if Joy came to Pittsburgh. Anyway, it would be impossible to stay in Selma's house, wrong to make love in Daniel's marriage bed.

But Joy's reluctance to welcome Daniel to her territory would be harder to excuse, if he asked. How to explain her satisfaction with the simple life she had constructed? How to explain its necessity? Not just because teaching, faculty politics, and the girls' demands left her drained as a juice box discarded on the cafeteria table. More than that: she breathed most deeply and easily alone, unobserved. She craved quiet evenings to read, listen to NPR.

Joy occasionally accepted colleagues' invitations to dinner but never reciprocated. The invitations grew rare. Joy did subscribe to the symphony with a colleague but enjoyed matinees at the movies or the theatre by herself, preferring to take in the show without worrying about a companion.

Joy feared that bringing Daniel too close would upset their homeostasis. She dreaded exceeding her capacity for intimacy.

Daniel tapped on her window.

He led the way around the horseshoe of cabins and unlocked their door. Joy stepped into unexpected warmth.

"I called and asked them to turn the heat on early." He knew Joy hated the cold; he paid attention.

Rosy light from an old fashioned pink pressed glass shade on the overhead light fixture softened the room and its simple furnishings. Joy stretched with contentment. Later, making love in the close darkness, she couldn't quite let herself go.

"Is something wrong?" he asked.

"Just tired."

"You know," he whispered, "I miss you more, seeing you more. I'm like a lonely dog in a crate, when I'm at home."

What to do if appetite generates appetite in one but not the other? What to do if one of us is a dog and one a cat? Stop overthinking, Joy told herself, curling against his warm back.

They drove in his car to the Lakeside Diner for breakfast. Joy finished first and went to the counter to have her thermos filled with coffee for later at the lake.

She returned to their booth. The stiff set of his shoulders alerted her, the cell phone on the table like a hand grenade.

"The home just called," he said. "She has pneumonia."

Every infection with Selma posed a potential crisis. And necessitated choosing whether to let nature take its course or to intervene. Daniel always chose treatment. Joy understood his futile determination sprang from love and guilt. And she respected his steadfastness, though it troubled her as well. Joy had never told him, but in Selma's circumstances, she herself would rather be allowed to die.

Selma was forty-four and could survive for a very long time. Wouldn't it be kinder to let pneumonia fill her lungs? Drowning couldn't be any worse than the nebulous drift of a persistent vegetative state.

"You told them to start the IV?" Joy asked the rhetorical question. He always instructed the home to pump Selma full of drugs to keep her here, or half here, or wherever she lingered. Now he would leave, drive back to watch over his wife.

"Not yet. I said I'd call soon. I'm not sure."

Startled, Joy tensed.

"Let's go to the lake," he said.

They parked in the deserted lot. Daniel retrieved his metal detector from the trunk; she slung her binoculars around her neck.

During warm weather they drove through the countryside, pursuing their respective hobbies. Daniel knocked on farmhouse doors, seeking out the owner in the barn if no one answered. Most granted permission for Daniel to wave his wand over their fields and the weedy margins beside the roads. He promised to show them what he found, to give right of first refusal. Daniel dug gently and meticulously refilled the small excavations. Once he found a button from the uniform of a Hessian soldier; the family didn't want it. He turned it over to the historical society.

No one minded Joy's birding. Occasionally a child tagged along. *What do you do with the birds after you've seen them?* Joy explained her life-list in the back of the Peterson's guide.

When, as now, hunting season made fields and forests dangerous, they prospected for birds and treasures in the protected zone of parkland around the lake. *Beach Closed* proclaimed the sign. Canoes lay chained and padlocked under the eaves of the concession stand; a layer of rough ice covered the water. The sand the rangers carted in each summer crunched underfoot, riddled with frost crystals. Ordinarily she could have left him on the beach, headed into the woods, and taken the woods trail around the lake. She would have enjoyed finding him again, afterward, refreshed by the break in togetherness.

But this morning the clock ticked back in Pittsburgh; the sand ran through the hourglass. The woman Joy had never met lay in the room Joy had never visited.

He hadn't turned the metal detector on. It lay on the sand like a discarded toy, an inert and powerless divining rod.

"What do you think?" he asked.

She exhaled a cloud of breath. "Do you want to call Monica?"

"I can't put it on her. Or you, for that matter."

Hunched against the wind he walked away. Joy almost followed but held back.

For once, she thought, Daniel needs to be alone.

He stopped by the stand of brittle phragmites and gazed at the lake.

Frozen drizzle stung her cheeks. Daniel needed her permission to give up. He might be able to let Selma go, and not blame himself too harshly, believing he'd done it for Joy, for the sake of their shared future. Joy could take the rap for him.

But what would happen to the two of them without Selma? Her absent presence held everything in balance, permitted Joy and Daniel's relationship to persist; forestalled or at least obscured the likelihood of entropy, of conflict, deterioration, and disorder. Removing Selma would disrupt their closed system, expose Joy's limited supply of energy and warmth.

He started back along the shore. She lifted the binoculars and twisted the eyepieces into focus to bring him close. Framed in her sights he appeared bruised with fatigue, old. Unable to bear it, she lowered the glasses.

I love him, Joy realized. The exception that proves the rule: loved him more than she'd believed herself capable.

Joy walked to meet him.

Mute, he shook his head. His eyes burned blank with anguish.

Joy cupped his face in her gloved hands. "You can say no. Tell them to keep her comfortable, but no treatment. Call Monica. Go home."

A quiet, jagged sob escaped him.

"I love you," she said.

She rested against his rough wool coat. Already Joy sensed a shift in their specific gravity—the ratio of her density to his, weighed in air.

Faith and Practice

Dorothy Shaw sat beside her husband Grayson, headmaster of Clear Spring Friends School, on the Elders' bench at the front of the Meeting House. His long fingers gripping his knees warned her. He was about to speak.

"I am wrestling with Spirit. True witness to peace must go beyond prayer. Action is called for. Civil disobedience. This Meeting must join in the effort to send medical supplies to North Vietnam. We must defy the government."

The members of Clear Spring Meeting disagreed over how far they should go in putting the Quaker peace testimony into practice; the Meeting was at war with itself. Grayson sided with the activists, the radical members of the Meeting. Although he was descended from one of Clear Spring's founding families, Dorothy worried that his provocative stance could alienate weighty Friends. The school was already in financial distress and needed the continued support of the Meeting.

Eight years earlier in this same room, Grayson had issued a different kind of challenge: "We of this Meeting are called to found a school." He'd persuaded Anna White, last in an old family, to donate her orchard and overgrown fields. At the regional Yearly Meeting, Grayson canvassed until enough money was promised to break ground. Clear Spring Friends School rose out of the fields across the road from the house where he had grown up, and where he and Dorothy still made their home.

At first, she'd just helped in the office. This role expanded into her present variegated one: admissions, counseling, discipline, surrogate mother to the boarding students. She could hardly tell where the job ended and she began. Peace in Vietnam was abstract compared to the welfare of the school. But Grayson was weary of the school's daily demands, restless. He'd been offered a job with a new peace organization, a radical splinter from the established Friends Service Committee. Dorothy had insisted he turn the offer down, telling him it was wrong to abandon the school before it was stronger. "You could run the school without me," he'd said. "No," she'd replied. Even after seventeen years, she was still an outsider in Clear Spring.

Now a student stood up in the balcony—Todd, a boarder from Florida. "This place is a bunch of hypocrites. All this crap about peace. They kicked my friend out of school this week. He's eighteen. He'll be drafted. Go ahead, send medicine to the Viet Cong. Send my buddy to war." He stamped downstairs and outside.

Todd's friend had been suspended twice the year before, for smoking. This time it was marijuana. "Strike three," Grayson had said, and expelled him. Dorothy was relieved to have him gone, though she hated losing his tuition.

There were nervous coughs as the Meeting settled back into expectant silence after the boy's outburst. To quiet her mind, Dorothy studied the plain, beautiful room, looking up at the heavy beam across the center of the Meeting House ceiling where the partition between men and women had been two hundred years ago. How shocked Grayson's ancestors would be at her students sitting in the balcony, holding hands. Across the room, the old glass in the windows warped the light, spreading it across the white plaster wall like a watermark on paper.

The benches creaked; the clock ticked. At the end of the hour, the clerk of the Meeting initiated the customary ripple of handshakes. Meeting was over; next came announcements.

"I'm driving down to the vigil," said Bruce Williams, the biology teacher. "Several students have already signed up. If anyone wants to go, we'll leave in the school van after coffee." Bruce drove to the silent vigil in front of the White House every Sunday. Sometimes Dorothy joined him.

Grayson scoffed at vigils. He said they were cheap and easy, too passive to truly convey resistance. "So how would you suggest we teach the children to bear witness for peace? Pour blood on files? Immolate ourselves?" she retorted. No one in Clear Spring had known the Quaker who recently had set himself alight in front of the Pentagon, but the tragic gesture haunted her.

From the broad porch of the Meeting House she watched a phalanx of honking geese fly overhead. There was smoke in the air, burning leaves. Standing here last April, after the impromptu Meeting called the night Martin Luther King was killed, it had seemed possible to smell the bitter smoke of buildings burning in the riots just fifteen miles away in Washington. The next Sunday she'd accompanied Bruce and his vanload to the vigil, driving past charred blocks and looted storefronts. Then, two months later, Bobby Kennedy was killed. All year violence had continued and escalated.

Her husband's cousin Sylvia joined them on the porch. "Do something about that boy. That's no way to behave in Meeting."

"He's young," Dorothy began, but bit back the defense. Sylvia sat on the Meeting's Finance Committee. "I'll speak with him."

Dorothy and Grayson started home through the cemetery. Most of those buried beneath mossy stones were his kin; she'd lie here one day, too, beside him. He opened the gate to the path through the fields. Runaway slaves had hidden here among the corn stalks, helped along their way to Canada on the underground railway by his grandparents. Sometimes, now, young men came to stay with members of the Meeting on their way to Canada, seeking a different freedom. Last year the Peace Pilgrim had appeared at Meeting one Sunday. The elderly woman had been walking back and forth across the country for fifteen years, since Korea, carrying out her vow to remain a wanderer until there was peace in the world. She stayed the night with them. After she left, Grayson had said she was engaged in a pointless exercise.

At the spring from which the Meeting took its name, two students were necking on the bench beneath the trees. Grayson chuckled. "It's not funny," Dorothy hissed. Students lolled against each other everywhere, it seemed. On campus she had to keep the music practice rooms locked or they were used for other kinds of practice.

"You know the rules about public display of affection," she called out in her sternest dean's voice.

"It wasn't public till you got here," the boy said, standing up and shaking back his long hair. It was Todd. He'd ignored her dress code; velvet bell-bottoms dipped beneath his jutting hipbones. Bright but a lazy student, he was especially popular with the girls. It was just a matter of time until she caught him with pot, too. His father, a real estate developer, was always proposing a "significant gift." The school had yet to receive a check or stock certificates. Was it a promise or blackmail?

The girl was Miriam Street. Dark hair and dark eyes, she looked like a gypsy in her long skirt made from an Indian bedspread. Her blouse was a skin-tight purple leotard, no bra. Dorothy would have to add underwear to the dress code; it seemed that nothing could be left to common sense or modesty.

Miriam was the child of another old Clear Spring family. Her mother, Garnet, had died that year. Garnet had been the first to befriend Dorothy when she moved from Philadelphia to marry Grayson. Soon the two women had been pregnant together, but Dorothy miscarried. She'd never conceived again; the friendship languished. Years later when Garnet became ill, Dorothy felt guilty, as though her envy of Garnet's healthy child had caused the cancer.

Miriam's father, Gil, a physicist, had recently lost his job with the Department of Energy over his participation in a vigil against biological weapons. Sometimes the price for bearing witness was too high. Since losing his wife and his job, Gil had been drinking and neglecting his daughter. Dorothy had convinced him to let Miriam come live on dorm, belatedly trying to make amends to the girl's deceased mother.

"I'll expect you both for Stewardship tomorrow," she said to Todd and Miriam. Students were assigned extra chores as meaningful punishment. Sweat equity, Grayson called it.

The boy smirked and grabbed Miriam's hand, lacing their fingers together. Dorothy itched to yank them apart. Insolent students infuriated her. Maybe it was just as well she'd never been a parent; at least she could leave the students and go home at night.

"It's time the two of you were heading back. We'll walk with you," said Grayson.

No one spoke as they tramped in double file, older couple behind the younger one, through the woods. They arrived at the rail fence where the school property began.

"Come have a bite with us, Miriam," said Dorothy. She'd rescue her from the predatory boy.

"Thanks, but I'll just go on back to the dining hall."

"I'll call the dorm, excuse you from lunch." The invitation had become an order.

"See you," said the boy, climbing over the fence instead of opening the gate.

The couple, Miriam in tow, crossed the road. The sign beside their mailbox read *Grayson Shaw, Cabinetmaker and Luthier.*

"What's a luthier?" asked the girl.

"Maker of stringed instruments," said Dorothy.

Grayson had been a woodworker before he started the school. Former customers still called, but there was no time for cabinetry. "Running a school is like running with a wild woman," he sometimes joked. He found time for his dulcimers only late in the day or at night. It was as necessary as breathing for him to be doing something with his hands.

Clear Spring's original music teacher, a young woman from South Carolina, had introduced the school to the lap dulcimer and inspired Grayson to try making one. "Can't carry a tune in a bucket," he said but attacked the project with enthusiasm and an engineer's precision.

He gave that first instrument to the teacher and she praised his gift for finding the voice in wood.

One morning Dorothy discovered an anonymous note in her mailbox in the faculty room. *Keep an eye on your husband the music lover.* She'd started to tear it up, but then tucked it beneath the blotter on her desk. At the end of the day, she passed it to Grayson across the supper table.

He read, rubbing his crew-cut hair. "Oh, for pity's sake. It's dulcimers I'm interested in, not that skinny little teacher."

Dorothy had looked around at faculty meetings. Who wrote the note? The music teacher left after just one year. Whatever else was true about what had happened, it was lonely at the school for a single woman.

The summer after, Dorothy and Grayson went dancing every weekend at the amusement park in Glen Echo. The prescribed steps, the physical closeness, eased the lingering wariness she'd felt. On the drive home she would rest her hand in Grayson's lap and sometimes they would end the evening making love. They won the waltz competition at the end of the summer, dancing with a sheet of paper pressed between them, paper pressed thin as the remaining shadow of her doubt. Grayson installed a wall of mirrors in his workshop, making it their private dance hall. They didn't use it now; after dinner most evenings there were meetings, student emergencies, paperwork, bills. But he still played the dance records when he worked on his dulcimers. Yesterday evening she'd come to the workshop to say good night and found him listening to a waltz as he stroked tung oil on the dulcimer with his softest brush (special ordered, made from the ear hair of Asian oxen). She'd thought for a moment of inviting him to dance, but it was too late, and it had been so long since they had been partners in that way. Grayson was right; the school was ravenous and absorbing. Not like a wild woman, but a demanding tribe of needy children. It was funny, that their shared work sometimes drew them together and other times pushed them apart. Perhaps parenting would have been like that, too.

"Show Miriam the dulcimer," Dorothy said now.

The workshop was fragrant with sawdust and varnish, Grayson's scents. Almost finished, the instrument lay gleaming on the bench. He used black walnut for the backs of his dulcimers, and spruce or red cedar for the tops, taking care to pair the slices of wood in book-matched sets, twin grains side by side, like open pages of a book. On this one, the top was red cedar. She thought spruce was prettier, but Grayson preferred the sound with cedar. Rich as chocolate, he said.

"The way it shines, it makes you want to touch it," said Miriam.

"Go ahead. It's the ruby shellac," he said. "Like rouge on a face."

Miriam traced the heart-shaped sound hole. Her fingernails were bitten to the quick.

"Let me show you what's inside." He always inscribed a fragment of verse in each instrument, beneath the sound hole. The poem had to be brief, the letters tiny, to fit. "You can read it if the light shines in just right," he said, holding the dulcimer up. "Can you make it out?"

The girl and the man stood side by side.

"The little rift within the lute by and by will make the music mute," the girl read.

Tennyson. Was he alluding to the intervals of distance between them? There was an intermittent, insidious fissure, a rip that had first opened years ago, after the failed pregnancy. For a long time afterward, making love seemed a dangerous obligation, freighted with the longing and the fear of conceiving again, which never happened. Eventually, she'd come to terms with being barren, her regret mitigated by taking care of him, and then of students. She'd comforted herself with the realization that there was at least sometimes a special closeness possible for childless couples.

The music teacher had ripped open the seam between them again. Though the ambiguous incident became woven into the warp and woof of the years, it left a flaw in the fabric. Recently, it had been his turn to be angry when she insisted that he stay on at the school. But over any long marriage, there were bound to be periods of equilibrium and disequilibrium, seasons of warm and cold.

"Why's it called a dulcimer?" asked Miriam.

"Latin," said Dorothy. "Dulce means sweet. Like the sound it makes. There's one in the house you can try. Please come help me with lunch."

"Give a shout when you're ready," said Grayson.

Autumn sunlight reflected off the kitchen's heart of pine floors. She kept the windows bare to see the trees in the orchard. But now the school had put the valuable land up for sale; it would be bulldozed for a housing development. She'd made her last batch of applesauce and stored it on the shelves Grayson had built for her in the cellar.

"You can set the table," said Dorothy. "Silverware is in the drawer of the sideboard in the dining room."

She telephoned the dorm advisor, one of their best young faculty, one they might lose next year to the higher salary of public school. "Miriam's having lunch with us," she explained. She arranged cold fried chicken from the evening before on a Blue Willow platter and poured applesauce into a pressed glass bowl.

"Which dishes should I use?" asked Miriam.

"The ones with the yellow flowers." The dishes had been part of her trousseau. *Use pretty things or you're in bondage to them,* her mother had said.

Miriam had seconds of everything: applesauce, devilled eggs, chicken. "Thanks, this was delicious."

"Thee must join us again," Grayson said.

Dorothy was startled. He rarely used the old Quaker form of address, except sometimes with her. It did feel right, having Miriam there. Without her, Dorothy might have criticized what he'd said in Meeting, accused him of further endangering the school. They would have quarreled. What if Miriam were to come live with them? It would reduce the cost of her scholarship to the school, and the girl would be safer here. They'd be safer, too.

"Lend me a dishtowel," said Grayson after lunch. Linen was best for rubbing in the final coat of carnauba wax. "And one of your nail files." Nothing better, he'd told her once, for getting around the curves on the body of the instrument. He left for the shop.

"Here's an apron," Dorothy said, tying her own. The apron's strings were getting shorter; she was thickening. She felt heavy beside the slender girl. "Why don't you wash, I'll dry and put away. There are rubber gloves under the sink."

Miriam plunged her bare hands into the soapy water. "I used to do the dishes with my mother. Dad lets them go till we run out."

"Your mother was my first friend, when I moved here."

"I miss her so much," said Miriam.

Dorothy was tempted to reach out and embrace the girl, but held back, always mindful of the necessary boundary between herself and students. "I'm so sorry," she said.

They worked side by side in easy silence. When the dishes were almost done, Dorothy forced herself to speak. "You must be careful, with Todd."

"We were just kissing."

"It's easy for things to get out of hand."

"It's no big deal, really. Are you going to tell my father?"

"No, I just want you to stop and think."

"I tried to talk to her about the boy," Dorothy said that evening, brushing her hair. "Keep an eye on her when you're on campus. I don't trust him."

"Too pretty for her own good. Just like her mother, when she was seventeen," said Grayson from the bed. He'd grown up with Garnet. Though it was foolish, Dorothy felt something like jealousy.

She crawled into bed beside him and reached for the Meeting's handbook, *Faith and Practice*. Tonight's passage spoke to her concern about Miriam, and the climate of casual physical affection between the students. The culture was so intemperate, lascivious.

"Listen to this. Maybe you could use this book in your class. It talks about sex in such a simple, good way."

Grayson taught Quakerism every fall, required of all new students. The course was really about his philosophy of life—how to mow a field, sand a board, how to find the Divine through work. He'd wanted to change the course this year, call it Activism. Dorothy persuaded him not to do that. But she had been encouraging him to include something about what the public schools euphemistically called Health. "The students look up to you," she'd said. "They might listen."

Now she read aloud. "Love is a relationship between people. The sexual encounter can be love and consecrate or it can be lust and desecrate."

"We don't use books in my class," he said.

She turned out the light; they did not reach out for each other, even in the dark. It was lonely in the bed without the weight of his arm across her. Sometimes they fell asleep on their separate sides of the bed and over the course of the night rolled close, warm animals seeking familiar comfort. But she knew even before closing her eyes that would not happen tonight.

The next morning Dorothy lay in bed, puzzling over the fragments of a dream. There had been a door in the bedroom opening to a secret room in the house. Lutes and viola da gamba hung from low rafters. A half-finished harpsichord stood in the corner. Maybe it was Grayson's dream slipping into her sleep, the way she sometimes found a stray wood chip from his hair on her pillow. He'd never made a harpsichord, never had the time. Perhaps he could, if he quit the school, took the job with the activists. If he were happier, would it set things right between them?

Later that day while taking a prospective student and his family on tour, she saw Grayson and his Quakerism class on the lawn in front of White Hall. He'd spread out an array of forked branches: peach, apple, pear. Students wandered across the grass like sleep walkers, branches held in stiff, outstretched arms.

"What are they doing?" asked the boy's mother.

Dorothy hesitated. This was the sort of thing people from outside misunderstood.

"Dowsing for water."

"What?" said the father.

"It's an old practice. If someone has the gift, the branch dips when you pass over underground veins of water. Watch, he's letting a student try with him."

It was Miriam. Today her leotard was peacock blue, but at least a vest covered her bosom. Grayson extended the branch; she grasped one fork, he the other. Holding hands, yoked together by the branch, they crossed the lawn. The stick writhed down.

"Cool," said the visiting boy. His father looked at his watch.

"This way," Dorothy said. "We'll visit biology now." The family wouldn't complete the application. Faith and mystery, and Grayson, were the heart of the school but their combination made it vulnerable, too. She should have known better than to linger here.

It was almost dinner time when she started home, taking the long way, around the pond and through the orchard. Last year students had sneaked in the night before the spring dance and ripped down blossoming branches. They smuggled the limbs back to decorate the cafeteria, transforming the ugly room into an enchanted forest. She'd overlooked the mischief since the trees were doomed anyway.

She heard waltz music from the workshop. Grayson must be finishing the dulcimer. She would ask him to dance, push herself across the gap between them; make peace. Dorothy opened the door.

Grayson pressed Miriam against the workbench, kissing her.

Adrenaline propelled Dorothy across the room. She pushed them apart; picked up the dulcimer and slammed it down.

Her husband groaned as the dulcimer cracked and splintered. She tossed the ruined instrument on the floor.

"Come with me," she ordered Miriam. The girl cowered behind him.

"Dorothy," said Grayson. "It's me at fault here."

"I know that. Come."

Dorothy had never intentionally destroyed anything before—except at the demolition derby at the county fair, soon after she'd married. Grayson bought her ticket; dared her. She'd swung the sledge hammer, smashing the car's windshield. Wrecking the car, such meaningless destruction, had been disgraceful but exhilarating. Grayson cheered from the sidelines.

At day's end, Dorothy liked to step into their quiet house but tonight, the tidy kitchen felt hollow and cold.

Miriam fidgeted with the cluster of wooden animals on the kitchen table.

"Leave those alone," Dorothy told her. The black walnut lion and the curly maple lamb had been Grayson's gift to her the first Christmas they were married. "Our peaceable kingdom," he had said. Every Christmas since he'd added to the couple's perennial centerpiece, carving animals from scraps of wood; this year's addition had been a basswood elephant.

"He was only going to show me how to dance. Are you going to tell my father?"

Dorothy imagined the smirks, the gossip in Meeting. Another humiliation, like she'd endured with the music teacher. Worse: this would be a scandal the school could ill afford.

"No, I'm not telling your father."

"Thank you," said Miriam.

Dorothy felt ashamed. Don't thank me, she should say. Don't listen to me. Don't lie.

"I'll walk you back to dorm."

After leaving the girl, Dorothy went to her office and sat at her desk, trying to collect her thoughts; trying, as Friends said, to reach clarity. But nothing was clear. The pain was worse now than when she'd discovered them—the way a burn hurts more after the initial shock. She locked herself in the faculty bathroom, turned the tap on full blast, and wept. Afterward, in the glare of the bare bulb over the sink, she stared at the mirror. How had she failed to notice that she'd grown old? She'd never tempt anyone again. Grayson and the school were all she had, all she'd have.

On her way home, Dorothy heard a car. Stepping into its path would give obliterating relief but she hesitated in the rough grass and the car swished by. Near the house she smelled smoke and discovered Grayson tending a small bonfire in the back yard.

"What are you burning?" she asked.

"The dulcimer. What's left of it."

The fire snapped and crackled between them.

"Perhaps it's time for you to take that job with the activists."

"You're sure, you're clear? That's what thee wishes?"

She stared at him across the flames. The heat of the blaze separating them felt good. That much at least was clear.

The Spring

She floated awake and remembered the note Jeff had left for her in the milk shed yesterday. Had he really asked her to come ride with him on the delivery run to the dairy? Jeff, a football star for the county high school, till he got hurt. She stared at the ceiling; Jeff smiled down at her, leaning out the window of his silver tank truck. Daddy surely wouldn't let her work for Cora if he knew she waited by the milk shed each day at the time Jeff picked up the milk.

Dawn seeped into her dark bedroom, softening it like a black and white photograph slowly washed with color, like the tinted high school portrait of her mother on the mantel. It was the only picture; her father disapproved of cameras, images. She studied it sometimes, wondering what the true colors of her mother's mouth, skin and eyes had been. Her own hair was the copper red of a scrub pad.

"Annie, you up?" Her father was at her door.

"Yes, I'm up." She made it true, pushing off the quilt.

"I'm going out to the goats. Call me when you've got coffee ready."

The stairs creaked, complaining under his weight. Annie sat up, swung her long legs over the edge of the bed, and tiptoed across the painfully cold wood floor to the bathroom. She studied herself in the mirror: light blue eyes, white skin, everything too pale except hair and freckles. She practiced flashing smiles for Jeff then hurried back to her room to put on her shirtwaist dress and sweater. Once at Cora's, she would change into jeans but her father preferred modest garb. She refused to wear a hair net.

Downstairs she flicked on the light in the kitchen, wishing for a radio to keep her company and tell of the weather and world outside the county. But he didn't countenance radios, even the Christian music station. Water boiled; she filled the drip pot. At least he still drank coffee. She watched little volcanoes erupt in the oatmeal cooking on the stove. Annie stepped onto the porch.

"Breakfast is ready," she yelled.

Back inside, she spooned oatmeal into bowls and poured two cups of coffee. Impatient to be on her way, she began to eat as her father came in.

"Wait a minute. We haven't asked the blessing," he reprimanded.

She put her spoon down. He washed his hands and stood by his chair, head bowed.

"Almighty God, we thy unworthy servants thank thee for our creation, preservation, and above all redemption. Amen."

"Amen," she echoed, grabbing up her spoon.

"Annie, never be in such a hurry that you neglect your prayers."

They began to eat in silence, his reproach twanging in the air above the table. He sugared his oatmeal heavily and added a big pat of butter.

"Cora called last night. Her basement flooded. Needs you to stay overnight and help clean up."

Annie kept her eyes down, not to appear too eager.

"Should I?"

"Long as you're back right after you do her chores tomorrow morning."

She finished breakfast and shot up the stairs for her nightgown, back downstairs to the kitchen. Still at the table, he stared into his empty bowl, shoulders slumped.

"You'll be alright here for dinner without me? There's meatloaf."

"Take a pie. She wanted apple. Make sure she pays for it, and for the extra time."

He resented her working out, even for an old friend like Cora, but they needed the money. She selected a pie from the pantry, leaving half a dozen for him to take to the bake shop.

"I'll be going now."

She hesitated on the door sill. He would be alright without her, wouldn't he?

He fixed her with his gray gaze as though taking aim. "Drive careful. God bless you." He looked away, releasing her.

Annie slammed free out the door and jumped into the old sedan. She opened the glove compartment and reached deep in, touching Jeff's note. Yes, it was real. She closed the glove compartment and turned the key in the ignition. The engine caught and she smiled, it had been unreliable these cool spring mornings. She hurtled down the rutted mud drive, past the rusty mailbox, flying up the ridge road to Cora's.

Mist rose out of the valley like boiling steam. Annie rolled the car window as far down as it would go and breathed in the moist morning. Bare branches in the woods blurred with new leaves, the hillside was painted with streaks of soft green. Annie would ask Cora the name of the white tree that was blooming all through the woods. Cora knew every wildflower and tree as well as she knew every family up and down the ridge. Annie pressed down the accelerator, racing over the last rise. Cora's big white barn stood strong and solid beside the road. The dogs barked as the car stopped; the setter bounded over as she climbed out. She knelt to tousle its ears. He'd been abandoned on Cora's porch not long ago, not unusual since everyone knew Cora never turned a stray away, but a lucky break for the setter. Short, sturdy Cora came down the porch steps, pushing aside her dogs.

"Morning, Annie." The warm smile stretched across her square-jawed, weathered face.

"Here's your pie."

"Take it on in. Meet you in the barn."

Annie found room for the pie on the crowded kitchen counter and went upstairs to change. She considered the spare room hers and kept a stash of nail polish and cosmetics on the vanity. Tonight she'd give herself a manicure, stripping it off like always before going home. Maybe take a bubble bath. Downstairs on the sun porch she slipped on mud boots. The setter tagged behind her across the road, whining when she shut him out of the barn. As her eyes adjusted to the dimness, she breathed in the warm scent of cow and hay dust and listened to the soothing stir and murmur of cows shifting back and forth.

"Back here with the calf," Cora called from the box stalls. She was on her knees beside the calf. Annie remembered the day it had been born, breech. The vet couldn't get there in time. Cora, bloody, triumphant, saved calf and mother, too.

"Looking good," Cora said as she slowly got to her feet. Annie helped her out of the stall. Back in the main barn they attached the milking machines.

"What's the pretty white tree all over the woods?"

"Sarvis. They say when the sarvis blooms, it's time to plant the oats. Another thing I won't get to this year," she sighed.

Annie hated her to talk like that. Cora was past sixty, older than Annie's grandmother had been when she died three years ago.

"Wish I could help you more."

"I get by."

Somehow farm people didn't, or couldn't, get old the way town people like her grandparents had. Cora just kept getting up every morning and doing what needed to be done.

Milking finished, Cora leaned on the fence by the small cemetery plot.

"Keep meaning to get a marker for Frank. They cost. Little Cora's pink peony is forty years old now, like she would have been."

Cora let the setter inside the house, but the rest of the dogs had to stay in the yard. The kitchen radio crackled, tuned to the local police channel. She said hearing the police reports made her feel safer. Annie wouldn't listen now to ambulance dispatches if she'd had a drunk husband die, like Cora's Frank, flipping his car over on the ice slick road two winters ago coming back from his night job at the turnpike. Cora poured coffee. Annie reached for a slice of toast.

Cora fiddled with the knob on the toaster. "This came out too light. Want yours down again?"

"No, it's okay. I don't like mine too crunchy."

Toast and coffee finished, Annie filled the sink with suds and washed the dishes.

"So, want me to start on the basement? Least it's sunny today, dry the stuff out." It was sure to be a mess. Cora's cellar had a dirt floor and was always dank and cold. Annie had seen mushrooms growing there.

Cora smiled. "Well, I told your Daddy a little white lie. There wasn't a flood. I asked for you to stay over so you can ride along with Jeff to the dairy like he asked you."

"He told you?"

"I told him to. The two of you, making eyes over the fence."

Annie stood very still at the sink, watching soap bubbles pop, one by one.

"I can't. Cora, you know I can't."

"Seventeen years old. Old enough to work right alongside me, and plenty old enough to go with Jeff if you fancy."

"But I don't know him."

"You spend some time together. Get acquainted. He's a good boy from good people, hauls the milk dependable. Might have got to college and played football if he hadn't busted his knee."

"Daddy wouldn't let me. You know how he is."

"Well, I know how he is now, and I know how he was when he met your mama in high school," Cora sniffed.

"What do you mean?"

"Your daddy just lost all interest in fishing and hunting overnight. They were crazy in love. Sometimes he'd bring her up here to visit awhile, then they'd run down that pasture to the woods like spring lambs."

Annie stared out the kitchen window, trying to see her grim father skipping down the meadow, crazy in love with a red-haired girl running beside him.

"He got religious to make up, when your mama died having you."

"Make up for what?" she asked, wary.

Cora vigorously ran a dishrag over the spotless oilcloth on the table.

29

"Make up for what?" Annie demanded, determined to get the answer.

"For loving too much, too soon. For not waiting to start you." She kept her head down, the gray curls in the home permanent Annie had helped her with seemed to bristle.

Loving too soon. Not waiting. "You mean they had to get married? I was a mistake?"

Cora's broad face crumpled like a ripe puffball mushroom after you stomped on it. The setter paced, toenails clicking on the scarred wood floor, and began to whine.

Annie exploded out the screen door and stumbled down the meadow behind the house, blinking in the sudden sunshine. She ran, trampling bluets and spring beauties in the grass. Safe in the shady woods she slowed down. The setter found her and bounded ahead, nose and tail quivering as he chased scents. She sat on a log and inhaled the loamy air. A woodpecker drummed on a tree trunk. May apples speared straight through last year's fallen leaves, white blossoms hidden beneath the green parasol of leaves. A few early trout lilies gleamed yellow. Purple violets bloomed by the stream.

Annie climbed down the bank to the water. She crouched, turning over rocks, startling hidden salamanders, searching out stones inscribed with the twisted trails of fossil worms. Once this had been the Appalachian Sea according to the geography teacher.

The setter splashed up the stream, shaking off wetness in a rainbow shower. He raced through the trees to the bright margin of the meadow. She followed to the edge of the woods. Cora's house perched at the distant top of the steep slope, like a ship sailing across a high green wave. What would it be like to sail away?

Cora's small figure appeared on the porch. Her voice wafted down the hillside.

"Annie, Annie. Come on up! Jeff's here!"

Annie fell back into the shadows. She paused beside the old walled spring where cows had been watered, before there was well water on the ridge. The spring was held on three sides by stone walls set into the hillside, a mossy hearth for water instead of fire. There was always water here, even on the late dry days of summer, mysterious water from the deep earth. She knelt and rested her head on her knees.

Leaves rustled. Annie froze still as a stalked deer. Footfalls crackled, a stick broke. From the corner of her eye she saw his work boots approach.

"Cora sent me. She's making tea," Jeff said.

She tried to answer, but her throat locked.

He knelt beside her. "Are you okay?"

Her eyes burned. She dropped her head between her knees, hunching her shoulders to strangle the tears. His hand touched her shoulder, gently. She held her breath. His hand traced circles on her back—wide, firm circles.

His arm cradled her; she rested on his flannel shoulder. He tipped her chin up, stroked a finger across her forehead and down her cheek. He kissed her. The sounds of the woods faded away. Liquid warmth spread inside her. His tongue slipped sweetly into her own mouth, his hand was moving down her belly. She felt as though a combination lock was being turned, tumblers clicking; she was opening. Then she pushed his hand away.

"No, I can't," she whispered, and pulled back.

"I'm sorry. It's just—I've been wanting to kiss you since I first saw you come out of the barn last winter."

She had never seen him before without his generous smile. He looked sad. Annie almost reached out to touch his lips.

The woodpecker drilled its lonely song. Jeff stood, brushing off his jeans, and held out his hand for her.

"We should get up the hill now. Cora's fixing to cut your pie."

"You go. I'll be along."

"What about that ride to the dairy? I won't bother you, I promise."

"No, I can't. Not today, anyway."

"Alright then. I guess I know how it is," he said.

31

She heard him walk slowly away. When he was safely distant, she looked up and watched him disappear, limping slightly, through the shade into the bright meadow.

Like a fish on a line drawn tight and tighter, she felt a sharp pain in her throat where a hook would lodge. Soon the line must break, or her throat would burst.

Annie peered into the clear, still spring. Her reflection stared back. She picked up a long stick and stirred the water fiercely, disturbing the mirror. Murky clouds of mud and debris swirled and slowly settled, like tea leaves in a fortune teller's cup.

She could not read any message in the clotted foliage floating in the water.

Surprise Boxes

The dean approved my petition to withdraw; I stripped my room in the freshman dorm. The Greyhound bus carried me home to Bedford through a freak April snowstorm.

I slept like a hibernating beast the first week and would have liked to sleep straight through the spring, hiding in my room, but my mother pushed me out of bed. Heavy and slow, as though walking underwater, I dressed and brushed my limp hair to please her. I felt erased, the past months flushed away without a trace.

"Enough moping. Go make yourself useful to Mr. Westervelt," my mother said.

It was easier not to refuse, so I walked to the church Mr. Westervelt had converted to his home and antique shop. He had retired and moved to town the year I was ten. *I'm a retired minister living in a retired church,* he liked to say. My mother said he had retired early and wasn't old, but he seemed old to me. His shop was my after-school refuge until high school. I abandoned him for drama club, year book and a summer job at the Frosty Bear selling soft serve ice cream to blond boys on the football team.

Now I walked through his church door again. The bell on the door-knob announced me just as always. He was reading at the cash register and put down his book. He looked more like Lincoln than ever, thin face and deep-set eyes, until he smiled.

"Margaret, my pearl," he said, as he used to. My name, he had explained, meant pearl in Greek, which he studied in seminary. "Your mother said you were home. Care to answer an old man's prayers and help out?"

"Okay," I said.

"Let's have a cup of tea before I press you into service."

We walked through the shop, dim and dusty as I remembered, and through the door behind the pulpit into his apartment, carved out of what had been the choir dressing room. I sat at his kitchen table and glanced around while he made tea. The bulky old phonograph was on its shelf in the pantry. I knew the piles of records on the floor were the popular songs from his youth. Glenn Miller. Frank Sinatra. "Dancing is my secret vice, Margaret. I'm thankful to be a minister, not a priest," he used to say. He had taught me to dance, on those afternoons, the year I was thirteen. Just before I went home for the evening, we would have our lesson. He was graceful, and had made me feel graceful as well, though I was growing tall too fast. He would lead me around the kitchen table and keep count as the music spilled and spun. My favorite song was *Fascination*. He had always played it last.

"Your tea, mademoiselle." He filled my china cup from the fat pot I remembered, snug in its knitted cozy, like a baby in a bunting.

He heaped sugar in his cup and stirred. It was like the old days when I used to sit at this table and sip milky tea—cambric tea, he called it— and eat graham crackers. He stroked his cat and we would talk. About customers, if he'd had any, and what they bought. About his missionary days in India. About my homework; we practiced the county seats of Pennsylvania, the presidents in order.

And now here we were again, drinking tea.

"You have perfect timing. I've just been to a big auction and could use help sorting."

My favorite task had always been sorting purchases from estate sales and auctions. Opening the cartons, unwrapping objects from layers of old newspaper had seemed like Christmas.

"Let me give you a tour, refresh your memory as to where things go."

The sanctuary was crammed with table linens, sheet music, books, buttons, old post cards, and costume jewelry. His inventory was always more junk than antiques, except for the glass-fronted cabinet of bone china. We paused there.

"I still have my weakness for fine china," he said. "Can't ever let a pretty piece go unclaimed, no matter if it's chipped or cracked. One man's trash is another man's treasure." Once I had been in the shop when a customer exclaimed, "Oh! This is my grandmother's pattern," as though her grandmother were restored with the pink-flowered saucer. It did seem possible, in the clutter of his shop, to find something precious that had been lost.

We squeezed down narrow aisles between laden card tables.

"Here are the salt and pepper shakers," he said. "I keep an eye out at the sales for the ones shaped like fruit, the ones you liked."

When I was his after-school helper, I had started a salt and pepper collection, purchasing one or two a week. He would have given them to me, but I preferred to pay, twenty-five cents a set.

He flipped on the light in the stairwell and I followed him upstairs. He paused on every step and leaned hard on the banister.

"The choir loft is still for clothes and hats. I put the everyday dishes, board games, jigsaw puzzles, and picture frames up here, too. When I can climb the stairs. My hip's a bit gimpy."

I spotted the old dressmaker's dummy he had rescued from a dumpster at the women's clothing store in town. We had named her Esmerelda. I used to dress her up in outfits culled from the cast-off clothes. Now she leaned in the corner of the choir loft, draped in an old wool coat with a fur collar.

"Esmerelda!"

"Yes, wish I was aging as gracefully as she. A classic beauty."

He made his painstaking way downstairs and sank into his chair by the cash register.

"Don't think I'm up for a trip to the basement today. Check it out. Then we can go to the garage and start work."

The basement was as I remembered: a dank catacomb of little rooms, packed with tools and pots and pans, coffee percolators, bottles, canning jars. I climbed back upstairs.

"Ready?" he asked.

"Ready," I replied.

"Well, no rest for the weary," he said, and hoisted himself out of the chair.

We walked through the shop and kitchen, out the back door into the garage. The big folding table he kept for sorting was covered with boxes.

"I've fallen behind. Glad you're here."

It was like old times. I fished in the cartons, handed each item over, and watched him deliberate before writing a price on a sticky circular label.

"This treasure is ready for the floor. Find it a spot. Remember, like goes with like," he said.

I did remember. It was a scavenger hunt in reverse, finding each piece its place. As I fell into the familiar quiet rhythm of working together, I recalled how I used to tell him about what I was reading. He sometimes had recited poetry. *Parting is all we know of heaven, and all we need of hell,* was the line that came back to me now, his voice in my mind's ear. I almost wanted to tell him what I had learned in college, about love. And ask him if he thought I would go to hell, for what I had done. But it was enough to work together until evening fell. Mr. Westervelt did not suggest dancing. I wondered, as I crossed the yards between his house and ours, if he could still dance, with his gimpy hip.

There was no letter waiting for me on the mail table. I had left a note, with my address, in his study carrel beside mine in the library, where we had first met, studying side by side. Once he had left a rose for me, on my books. I had the dry petals in my jewelry box. He had been avoiding the library, before I went away, before I conveniently disappeared. He would not write.

"I'm back here," called my mother from the kitchen. I walked down the hall.

"So, how was your day?" she asked, scanning my face with a quick glance.

"Okay."

"Did he tell you the doctor wants him to have hip replacement?"

36

"He didn't mention it."

I went back the next day.

"Margaret, my pearl," he greeted me, as though I were the person he most wanted to see in the world. "There's a good sale advertised in *The Gazette*. Let's go." He hung the *Closed* sign in the window and locked the door. Early spring was quiet, no need to worry about missing customers.

"Be my chauffeur, please."

Driving his dilapidated station wagon, my attention on the twists and turns of the road, the cotton fog in my mind cleared. The quiet road unrolled. Tree branches were misted with the first green leaves. We rode past red barns emblazoned with *Chew Mail Pouch Tobacco, Treat Yourself to the Best* and big metal mailboxes planted hopefully by the end of long drives leading to weather-beaten farm houses.

We came to the sign: *Sale Today.* I followed the arrow and parked in the mud beside a rambling house.

"Ah, the thrill of the chase," he said. "You go in first. Case the joint, I'll let your young bones do the leg work. Come back and tell me what to bid on, and who is going to outbid us."

There was little there but musty rooms and dust. Scarred furniture. Battered suitcases and stained chenille bedspreads. An empty playpen. And potholders like giant mittens. Potholders like the ones that had been slipped over the metal stirrups on the clinic table, to cushion my cold feet during the procedure.

"Not much," I told him, returning to the car.

"Well, no matter how slim the pickings, I'll find something." Mr. Westervelt bought something at every auction, out of sympathy for the family. That day he bid on sealed cardboard boxes labeled *Kitchen, Dining Room,* and *Bedroom.*

Back at the store, we worked as a team, sorting the flotsam and jetsam from the cartons. He perched on a step stool while I spread the contents out on the table in the garage for his inspection. It was mostly junk. But he said, "For every sock there's a foot." He priced the saleable merchandise, writing neatly with a fine tip felt pen. I found each piece

37

its spot, like with like, in choir loft, sanctuary, or basement. The dregs, like an electric curler set missing some rollers, went to the picnic table under the garage eaves. *Help Yourself* said his hand lettered sign. These offerings always vanished, the way giant zucchini disappear overnight from give-away produce stands.

Finally, only little things remained on the sorting table, too good to give away, too insignificant to sell. Old fashioned white gloves. A pair of dice. Souvenir pens and pencils. Macramé plant hangers. Packages of complimentary greeting cards from charities. Hotel soaps, shampoos and body lotions. Plastic toys from fast food meals. He used these left-overs like crackerjack prizes to fill empty shoeboxes, labeled in his neat block printing: *Boy's Surprise Box; Girl's Surprise Box; Lady's Surprise Box; Gentleman's Surprise Box.* Each cost a dollar, and his sign beside them read, "The odds are good, but the goods are odd."

His surprise boxes were special favorites in summer when the camp-grounds by the lake filled with families out from Pittsburgh. He let sunburnt children heft each box before choosing. "No shaking, and no peeking, until you're out of the store. No refunds, and no returns— unless you find I've put in a hundred-dollar bill by mistake," he warned the small customers. The children would hand over crumpled dollar bills and race outside to crouch at the foot of the stairs and open the cardboard treasure chests.

Now, he selected items for next summer's boxes with tender con-centration and tied the lids shut with twine. A diaper pin with a pastel plastic clasp shaped like a duck caught my eye; I slipped it in my pocket.

The next week, scouting at another auction, I found a bride's dress: size eight, tags still on from Kaufmann's in Pittsburgh. The veil was there too, wilted on the hanger. And a pair of satin pumps, soles pristine. I went out to the car where he was waiting.

"A bride's dress, never worn."

"The wedding must have been called off. Like mine," he said, sur-prising me.

"What happened?"

"We'd have to ask the bride, and she's not here."

I mean what happened to you, I wanted to say.

He limped over to the folding chairs set up in front of the auctioneer. I sat beside him.

"It's a lovely dress," he said, when it came on the block, and bid on it, surprising me again. There was no competition. Antique dealers were not interested in a bride's dress only a few seasons out of fashion.

"The two of you planning to tie the knot?" the auctioneer teased.

I blushed. Mr. Westervelt shook his head and smiled.

At the store, I unloaded the ivory satin dress, tulle veil, and pumps along with the more usual cargo of dishes, ice skates, and old *National Geographic* magazines. In a carton of books there was a battered copy of *Dr. Spock's Baby and Child Care.* I started to read. *Trust yourself. You know more than you think you do. Soon you're going to have a baby.* I dropped the book back in the box.

He priced the dress, veil, and shoes last, as a package: twenty dollars. Putting down his pen he said, "Think I'll take a lie-down. Go on home, thanks for your help."

"I'll stay and finish putting the stuff out."

"If you want, thanks."

He walked through the door behind the pulpit into his apartment.

I busied myself, finding places for the new items, like with like. My eye fell on the bride's dress, gleaming in the jumble. It was unlike anything else in the store. I supposed it should go to the choir loft, where the old clothes were. I stroked the folds and picked it up. The gown filled my arms, heavy and smooth. I started upstairs then sat on the steps, cradling the dress, the lustrous satin pooled on my lap. The shop was quiet, mid-week quiet. No one would come in. I went upstairs and laid the dress down gently on the floor. In the dim loft, the gown shone like moonlight on water, tempting me with the promise of smooth satin on my skin. Kicking off my sneakers, I stripped out of my jeans and T-shirt. I stepped into the dress and pulled it up. It was stiffer than I had expected; I could not fasten the tiny buttons down the back. Holding up the full skirt, I walked downstairs to see my reflection in the full-length mirror beside the pulpit. The white satin dress transformed me the way snow hides and heals the everyday world.

The door behind the pulpit opened and Mr. Westervelt stepped into the shop.

"Oh, Margaret. Aren't you lovely." He held out his hand to me. "May I have this dance?"

I followed him into the kitchen. He put *Fascination* on the phonograph and took me in his arms, his hand warm on my bare back where the dress gaped open. We waltzed around the kitchen until the song ended.

"You will be a beautiful bride one day," he said. I drank in his words like a blessing and a promise, as though he could forgive me for the sin he did not even know and foretell a happy ending.

I changed in his bathroom, reluctant to take off the dress and put on my ordinary clothes. I carried the heavy armload of satin back to the shop. Mr. Westervelt was standing by the cash register.

"Bring down Esmerelda. Let's have a bridal display," he said.

I dragged the mannequin from the choir loft. He brought a washcloth, towel, and bar of soap from the apartment and washed her blind, scratched face.

"You dress her, for decency's sake," he said, smiling.

She was built like a giant Barbie, pointy bust, wasp waist, and arched feet, perpetually on tiptoe. Stretching her out on the floor, I wrestled the gown on, then tipped her upright. The veil covered her baldness, softening her pocked face. I propped her up by the pulpit under the stained-glass window.

The bell on the church door jingled. A girl came in. I recognized her; she sold pies at the bakeshop by the turnpike exit near town. She looked about my age. Her red hair was scraped back from her high forehead in a tight ponytail, pulling tissue-paper thin skin taut.

"Hello there. Thanks for stopping in," he said.

She glanced at the mannequin and turned away.

"Do you have any plain dishes? I'm looking for Corelle ware."

"Take a peek upstairs. Might be some," he said.

The stairs squeaked as she went upstairs. Then it was quiet again, except for muffled clinks from the choir loft. She came down with a couple of place settings of white dishes and took them to the cash register.

"You don't have any pots and pans, do you?"

"In the basement. Put the light on, you're the first today."

She returned with an old drip coffee pot, a double boiler missing the lid, and a cast iron skillet.

"Looks like you're setting up house-keeping," he said.

"I'm getting married."

"Congratulations." Mr. Westervelt stroked the cat in his lap.

"That's a pretty dress over there," she said.

"Would you like to try it on?"

"I'm not having a church wedding."

"Try it on, why not?"

She shook her head, gazing at the dress.

"Margaret, slip the dress off Esmerelda and show this young lady where my bathroom is. She can change there."

I struggled the dress off the mannequin. My fingers were clumsy and slow; my head buzzed. Cradling the dress in my arms, I led the girl into his apartment. She followed so close behind me she stepped on the heel of my sneaker. I turned on the light in the bathroom, surrendered the dress, and left her alone. I went back to the shop. Soon, I heard the whisper of heavy fabric. The girl stood beside the pulpit. Late afternoon sunlight streamed in the stained-glass window, a halo of dust motes danced around her. The dress and the girl glowed. My eyes stung.

"It has your name on it. Slip out of it and we'll see what I've got in the way of a box," he said.

"I couldn't."

"You'll be doing me a favor, get it off my hands. Not much call for bridal gowns in a store like this. Take it as my wedding present."

I swallowed. The back of my throat burned.

"Thank you," the girl said.

She swirled around, graceful as a Fall Foliage Festival Princess, and vanished into the apartment.

Mr. Westervelt opened a Lady's Surprise Box.

"Margaret, look in the jewel case and pick out some nice earrings for our bride."

The display of costume jewelry was half hidden behind the rack of old postcards. There was a pair of luminous pearl drops, perfect for a bride. I selected a different pair, rhinestone clips. He wrapped the earrings in a scrap of tissue and put them in the box. Then he opened the cash register drawer, took out a twenty, folded it, and tucked it in. He closed the box and retied the string.

In a few minutes she returned and laid the dress and veil beside the cash register. He folded the gown into a box and laid the cloud of veil on top.

"Hang it in the bathroom after a shower, steams out the wrinkles."

He wrapped the plates and cookware in old newspapers, put them in a shopping bag, and rang up her purchases. She paid. Then he put the Lady's Surprise Box in the bag.

"A little something for the bride, no extra charge, and no returns."

She slipped the shopping bag handles over her thin wrist, picked up the dress box and held it close. The bell on the door rang as she went out.

I hauled the mannequin up to the choir loft and found her a flowered housedress. He was reading by the cash register when I came downstairs.

"I'll be going now."

"Thanks for your help. A good day's work."

Walking home, I fingered the pearl earrings in my pocket. I hid them away in my jewelry box, with the diaper pin, and the rose petals.

Antiques and Collectables

"A girl in trouble here in the country is really in trouble, worse than in town," he told the couple, former parishioners who drove out from the city to seek his help. "Place an advertisement. You could be the answer to each other's prayers."

He had married them while still pastor of his church in Greensburg, his last wedding before he retired to the country to run an antique store housed in a former church: merchandise in the sanctuary, living quarters honeycombed behind the pulpit. "I am not leaving the church, I'm moving into it. I am giving up salvation work for salvage work," he had joked in his retirement homily. A minister never really retires. He substituted in the Methodist pulpit in the village and in summer served as chaplain at the lake campground.

The couple composed an advertisement with the desperate hope a castaway invests in the note tucked in a bottle. They paid his local paper in advance to run it weekly, all summer. The woman called him the first Sunday in July, just before he left to preach.

"Is the ad in?" she asked, voice brittle and bright.

"Right at the very top of the Classifieds."

"I am praying. But should I pray for someone else to have misfortune?"

He would be late. He did not have time for her qualms.

"Dear, you will be the way out of misfortune for some poor girl," he said, balancing the phone on his shoulder as he buttoned the clerical collar around his thin neck.

He gathered his sermon notes; his fishing rod and tackle box were already in the car. Reverend Westervelt hurried along the road to the lake and stopped at the bait shop, open early even on Sunday mornings, to purchase night crawlers. He put the worms in the cooler in his car. Every Sunday after the service he drove to the dock where he kept his rowboat, unbuttoned his dog collar, and went fishing.

Preaching at the campground had proved an unexpected delight. The amphitheater beside the lake was carved into a hillside shaded by hemlock. Evenings, park rangers gave talks on stargazing and bird identification. Sunday mornings, standing at the podium to preach, with his back to the lake, he thought of those first outdoor sermons in Galilee, not that he was confusing himself with Christ. He kept the service short and sweet, opening prayer, homily, closing prayer. It was ministry with no strings attached—no collection plate, no elders to please, a choir of bird song rather than a prima donna music director. Best of all, there were different faces every week, no obligation to become involved. The temporary, transient congregation of vacationing families was always relaxed, cares left behind. They reminded him of the saying carved on the sundial his congregation had given him as a retirement gift: *Count only the sunny hours.*

This morning one congregant did not fit in. She sat on the last bench, the only solitary among the family groups. A bruise bloomed across her face, livid even from where he stood. The service ended.

"Amen. Peace be with you," he said.

The families filed out to go swimming, fishing, bicycling.

But she sat still. He sighed; he would have to stop and speak to her. On the lake, the early mist had cleared, the water sparkled its invitation. The first fishermen were out but he would have to wait. He was an ordained fisher of men, mandated to stop for emergencies of the soul just as a doctor must stop at car accidents. There might be no fishing this morning. He hoped he would remember to put the night crawlers in the refrigerator when he got home. He walked the sandy aisle to the last row. She sat, head bowed, face hidden. If he had not seen the bruise earlier he could have just murmured, "Bless you," and walked on.

"Can I help you, my child?"

She looked up. He recognized her. She was the girl who had come into his shop a while back. She had bought dishes, tried on the old wedding gown and taken it also. Now the bruise branded her lovely face, her nose and cheeks were swollen. Her pale blue eyes were puffy and bloodshot.

"I remember you from the shop. How are the wedding plans coming along?

"I'm not getting married."

"Your boyfriend hit you?"

"My father, when he found out about my boyfriend." She began to cry.

"Here." He handed her the handkerchief he kept ready in his hip pocket for pastoral emergencies and looked out at the smooth, shining lake and at the green hill, gently rolling back from the far shore. *I will lift up my eyes to the hills from whence cometh my help.*

"I was about to go fishing. Come along."

She drew a breath. "I like fishing."

"Good. That's two of us. I'm Reverend Jim Westervelt."

"I'm Annie."

They spent the morning on the lake. He caught a couple of smallmouth bass. The girl seemed comforted by the gentle rocking of the flat-bottomed boat, by the warmth of the sun. He thought of hours wasted in his church study, counseling the weary and heartbroken. It would have been better to just take them fishing.

"My boyfriend says there's someone over in Cumberland who gets rid of babies."

"Is that what you want to do?" he asked, eyes on his line.

"No," she whispered. "My mother didn't get rid of me."

He gazed into the deep green water of the lake and remembered rowing across the blue water of Lake Maggiore with Michaela, the last afternoon together almost fifty years ago. She had been crying, unable to defy her mother and priest to marry a Methodist soldier from America. So, the war over, he returned to Pittsburgh without a dark-eyed Catholic

45

bride to explain to his own mother. He lost himself in seminary studies, but in his narrow bed at the end of long days, he had ached for Michaela. Some of his fellow seminarians did marry, but it seemed God's will that he be solitary.

His congregation became his family. He ministered to them in their joys and sorrows, and they cared for him as well. But finally, it had been a relief to retire and put down the millstone of so much caring. Now that he was free, needed by no one, memories of Michaela sometimes returned, disturbing his peace like breeze across the still surface of the lake. He glimpsed Annie's reflection in the water. What if Michaela had discovered she was pregnant, after he left? He might be a grandfather, even a great-grandfather now.

"It's getting hot," the girl said. Her fair skin was beginning to burn, pink framing the purple margins of the bruise.

"We should go in." He rowed toward shore.

"I can't go home."

"Is there someone you might stay with?"

She shook her head. Tears spilled down the sunburnt skin. "Cora— the woman I was working for—she died."

Was God prompting him? Testing him? He was too old to play Samaritan. "Well, stay with me, help in my store. While you figure things out."

He watched her battered Buick in the rear-view mirror follow him along the road, past the ranger's station, past the bait shop. He was accustomed to bringing back treasures from country auctions for his shop. What was he bringing home this time?

Reverend Westervelt opened the sofa bed in his study and laid out linens. He found antibiotic cream in the bathroom and brought it to her.

"For your face," he said, holding out the tube.

She looked up from making the bed. He imagined sitting on the edge of the bed, drawing her down onto his lap, and anointing her wounded face. The strangeness of the situation struck him full strength. If he were not seventy years old, this would be improper.

"The bathroom is down the hall," he said and retreated to the kitchen to clean the fish.

She followed and sat at the table: a golden old oak pedestal table, one of his best finds. Every now and again he came across something he couldn't part with.

"How about a fish fry for lunch?"

"No, thanks. I'm not hungry."

The Gazette lay on the table. He pushed it aside. "Where's your father's place?"

"You going to tell Children and Youth?"

"How old are you?"

"Eighteen."

"Anyone else at home he might hurt?"

"No. He never hit me before."

He doubted she was eighteen, and the rest might be a lie, too.

"What about getting your clothes?"

"I brought some things in my car."

"Let me call your boyfriend. The three of us could talk."

Hope blazed in her eyes.

"Give me his number, please. There's paper by the phone."

She wrote the number down. "I don't want to be here, when you call. Could I—could I take a nap? I didn't sleep last night at all."

"It's Sunday afternoon. Napping is the traditional activity."

She smiled, but the smile did not touch her eyes, just stretched her wounded skin. He wanted to embrace her, to ease her pain—just reflex after years of offering comfort. He turned to the sink as she left the room.

He washed the fish scales from his hands, hung up his denim apron, crossed the room to the phone and lifted the receiver. The dial tone buzzed; he hung up. Better to wait, let the girl rest. Let the boy come to his senses and miss her. No hurry. He would not mention Annie to his couple in Greensburg yet. He might help the girl and her boyfriend work things out, or he might find another plan. Someone might come

47

forward she could stay with, someone who would help her keep and raise the baby. You never knew; someone like that might turn up. "For every sock there's a foot," as he said to customers.

He breaded the fish in corn meal, fried the fillets, and garnished them with a little lemon and parsley. He carried his plate and a glass of ice tea into the courtyard garden behind the old church and balanced the dishes on the broad arm of the Adirondack chair. The chair had been another good find on one of his foraging trips. Before sitting down, he picked a sprig of mint for his tea from the herbs by the sundial. He settled into the chair and said grace aloud as was his custom, even though there was no one to listen except his cat, aged and dozing in the sun.

"Gracious heavenly Father, we thank Thee for this day. We thank Thee for the blessings and opportunities Thou hast given us."

A baby should be a blessing and an opportunity. What a shame her circumstances occasioned sorrow rather than joy.

He sat in the sunlight and ate with simple animal content. Finished, he went indoors and found the door to the study (her room now) closed. Was that soft weeping? Should he comfort her? He held the porcelain doorknob until it grew warm in his hand; he let go and turned away.

Reverend Westervelt washed his dishes, soothed by warm water and the citrus scent of detergent. He polished the plate dry and swept the kitchen floor. Tidying the table, he tossed the newspaper and the scrap of paper with the boy's number in the trash. Really was no need to call. Her Buick parked here was as good as an advertisement in *The Gazette* regarding her whereabouts. The boy could find her, if he wanted. And no reason to be hasty about bringing her together with his childless couple. Eternal souls, born and unborn, were at stake. He should take his time deciding what would be best for everyone. He wiped the table as Annie came in.

"What did he say?"

"I wasn't able to reach him."

That evening they carried folding lawn chairs to the field behind the firehouse for the Little League game. She sat close; he breathed in the mingled scent of sweat and shampoo. After the game the firemen set off fireworks. She gasped each time a rocket shot up, sighed as the waterfall of sparks fell to earth. He remembered Michaela's soft exclamations at climax and his face burned in the dark.

"That was beautiful," she said as they walked home.

"I always like fireworks."

"I never saw them before."

"You don't go to the lake to see the show on the Fourth?"

"My father doesn't like to."

Next morning, she was still asleep when Reverend Westervelt stepped outside with his grocery list and library books.

"Another scorcher," his neighbor called from her garden.

"Anything you need in town?"

"No, thanks, Reverend Jim. I'll have some tomatoes for you later."

His knees too stiff for garden work, he only maintained the few herbs around the sundial: mint for tea, parsley and thyme for omelets. The neighbor kept him well supplied with garden vegetables in season. He'd officiated at her husband's funeral two years ago. Sometimes now he suspected she had more than a neighborly interest in him. Always careful not to confuse pastoral care with personal affection, he knew from experience some lonely women were attracted to men of the cloth.

Reverend Westervelt drove through the village, passing the Methodist church, then the fire station and Evelyn's Market. Campers from the lake used the market but the selection was limited and expensive. He preferred to drive to town, visit the library, shop at the Food Lion. The town was the county seat and still some blocks possessed a fading elegance. The two hotels were closed now; one converted into a rest home. Beyond the town limits a couple of resort hotels remained. One had been famous, but its mineral springs were silting up and though the golf course was still open, the place was on borrowed time.

The library was on the first floor of a fine stone house on Juliana Street. He entered the gracious, well-proportioned foyer and admired the sparkling fanlight over the paneled door and the sweeping stairs to the second floor where the historical society had its office and the librarian lived. He occasionally ate dinner with the librarian in her high-ceilinged dining room before attending concerts at the Episcopal Church. She hesitated to retire since it would mean giving up her apartment. It would be like leaving a parsonage.

Alone in the non-fiction section in what had been the back parlor, Reverend Westervelt scanned the shelves to find what he needed. Selecting *Childbirth Without Fear*, he slipped the volume into his book bag. Not stealing—just protecting the girl's privacy—he would place it in the book drop early one morning.

Returning to the front parlor, he spun the crime carousel and chose several paperback mysteries at random.

"Didn't find what you were looking for back there?" the librarian asked.

"Just browsing."

Children trooped in, noisy and rambunctious; she did not press him and he slipped outside.

At Food Lion, he rolled his grocery cart up and down the aisles, adding whatever Annie might need or might tempt her: milk, chicken noodle soup, junket. It cost more than usual at checkout, but his pension went more than far enough out here. Besides, who was he saving it for?

He stopped for corn and watermelon at a roadside stand. Once home, he discovered a pick-up truck parked beside Annie's car. He felt the twinge in his chest, the shortness of breath. Mitral valve prolapse, his doctor said. *Your warranty is wearing out, Jim. You need to do a stress test.*

Leaving the groceries in the car he hurried inside. Where was she?

He found them out back in his Adirondack chair: a boy with Annie on his lap, a tangle of blue denim and shining hair. Reverend Westervelt cleared his throat.

She jumped up.

"This is Jeff."

The boy unfolded from the chair, tall and skinny.

"Pleased to meet you. Perhaps you could give me a hand with my groceries."

Annie and the boy made quick work of the task. Brown bags covered the kitchen table.

"Thank you. Some liquid refreshment?"

"Just about to take Annie for a drive."

"If you don't need me," she said.

"Before you go, let's chat."

"It wasn't me that hit her," the boy said.

"That's not what we need to talk about."

"The rest is between me and her. Coming?" he asked the girl.

Annie followed the boy to his truck, not looking back.

Reverend Westervelt put away the groceries and went back to the car for the books. The door to his study was open. He picked up her hairbrush from the bureau, pulled a strand of curly red hair from the bristles, rolled it between his fingers. The wedding gown from her original visit to his shop gleamed in the dark closet like a satin ghost between a denim skirt and a cotton shirt. Had she been keeping the gown hidden in the trunk of her car? It touched him to think of her driving around with it, as though she might need it at any moment. He laid *Childbirth without Fear* on the pillow beside her soft worn flannel nightgown.

He poured a glass of ice tea and went into the shop, flipping the cardboard placard in the church vestibule from *CLOSED* to *OPEN*, unlocking the door. No need to turn on the lights until the first customer, pleasant to rest in the dim filtered radiance of the stained-glass windows. He sank into his armchair behind the cash register.

Shop keeping was easy, compared to ministry. It reminded him of presiding over a perpetual church supper, his only responsibility arranging other people's offerings for a potluck buffet. Customers grazed through tools and kitchen implements in the basement, books and fine china on the main floor, every day dishes and old clothes in the choir loft. The shop's modest proceeds went to *Save the Children* for the South American orphan he fostered. Her sad dark eyes looked down from a framed photograph on the wall by the cash register, above the rack of self-published booklets of his sermons and poems.

He relished the quiet expectancy of the shop, welcomed whoever came and admired whatever they purchased. Summer days were busy with fishermen's wives sifting through kitchen utensils and children bicycling from the campground for his surprise boxes of trinkets and junk. Today he looked for Annie each time the bell on the door jangled. Well before five, he flipped the sign to *Closed* and locked the door.

Reverend Westervelt stood in his empty, quiet kitchen. Someone rapped on the back door. He hurried to answer and found only the neighbor lady.

"The big boys have come in!"

It took him a moment to realize it was the green cardboard punnet of tomatoes she referred to, not a bunch of kids.

"How's it going with your company?" she asked, peering around him into the kitchen.

He hesitated. "She's helping me out quite a bit."

"Might need more than a bit of help herself. Father's strange."

"She's here to get away from him."

"Just mind what you're getting into."

The tomatoes glowed red on the table. He sliced into one, releasing a warm flood of seeds and juice. He fried the bacon the doctor had forbidden and made a sandwich. The evening wore on. He tried to read but kept glancing at the clock. Long past midnight; slumped half asleep in his chair, he roused. The truck, at last!

Her face was flushed. She perched on the arm of his chair. He caught a whiff of beer; she was tipsy. There was also another sweet, musky scent he remembered from long ago. His heart twinged.

"Last chance to see him for a while. He's taken a job truck driving. It's really good money. When he comes back, we'll get married."

It was hard to fall asleep with Michaela and Annie floating in the dark above his bed, like seraphs painted on an Italian church ceiling, cherubs above the velvet seats of the movie theater. The ache of yearning caught him by surprise. Ashamed, helpless, he slipped his hand beneath the covers.

At breakfast her eyes looked tarnished; the hopeful gleam of the night before vanished. "I should go home. My father needs me."

He could let her leave; reclaim his solitude. But the father was violent; the boy might convince her to visit some back-alley abortionist.

"I'll call Children and Youth if you go." Not threatening, not meddling—just guiding and protecting; doing his job. A minister never retires, after all. Not with health and safety and immortal souls at stake. "Think of the baby."

"I can't stop thinking. I am sick of thinking."

She stayed. He taught her to run the cash register, keeping her occupied, soaking up the restless despair. Keeping her safe.

The next morning as he prepared to go to an auction, she offered to mind the store. He did not dare leave her behind alone. Her father might kidnap her. The boy might lure her to take to the road with him.

"Drive for me. My hip's bad today," he said, handing her the station wagon keys.

At the sale he bought an old walnut cradle, spending more than he intended, almost losing it to a big city dealer.

"It's beautiful," she said, shy.

"Not yet. Will be." He would strip the varnish, rub the thirsty wood with linseed oil.

A battered pick-up truck missing a bumper was parked by the church. A bearded man in baggy overalls leaned against it.

"My father!" She gripped the steering wheel so hard her knuckles whitened parking the station wagon beside her car.

Reverend Westervelt walked toward the man, extending his hand.

"Good afternoon."

He ignored him, addressing his daughter who stood barricaded between the station wagon and her car.

"Time you got back home." He stepped toward her.

She jumped into her car, backed out, and sped toward the lake.

The man dropped a paper bag on the station wagon's hood. "Better not put a hand on my girl."

"Get off my property," Reverend Westervelt said. "Now."

Before unloading the other auction purchases from the station wagon, he carried the cradle to his workshop in the garage and began to strip the old varnish. He left the shop closed and worked all afternoon until he heard her car pull in.

"Your dad left that for you," he said, pointing to the paper sack on the hood of his car.

She drew out a framed photograph. "My mother," she said, holding it out.

"You resemble her."

"Hope I don't die having this baby like she did with me."

He could not catch his breath over the sharp pain in his chest.

"You won't. But we should find a doctor for you."

"No one can know till Jeff's back. Till we get married." She sounded fierce, as if saying it to make it true.

Headlights woke him. A door slammed. He braced himself. He should get up. He lay tense, waiting. Whoever it was pulled away. He turned over in bed, changing hips, and fell back to sleep.

In the morning he found the church steps and his yard littered with underpants and brassieres. Huge white letters scrawled out "WHORE" across the side of her car. "PERVERT" was painted on the church door.

His neighbor watered her tomatoes without calling out a greeting.

Reverend Westervelt stooped to gather the undergarments, shameful to touch the intimate apparel, but clearing the mess before Annie woke.

54

He couldn't spare her seeing the words on her car and the door. She worked beside him to paint out the filth, tears streaking down her face. Afterward she went to her room and refused to come out even for lunch.

He was in the garage working on the cradle when a sedan pulled up. A thin blond woman climbed out.

"Good afternoon," she said. "I'm Mrs. Beal, from Children and Youth. There's been a complaint, that you are harboring a minor here, that there's been some disturbance."

"I'm providing sanctuary to a child who's been abused."

"I need to speak to the girl. In private."

He left her in the kitchen.

"Annie," he called through the door. "You need to come out. There's a lady here to see you."

"You promised not to call them."

"I didn't. Talk to her. We'll sort it out."

He sank into his chair behind the shop counter, hunkered down in his foxhole until Annie came.

"She wants you now. She made me show her the apartment. Your room, mine."

He entered his own kitchen as though called to the principal's office. The woman sat at his table.

"Please sit down," she said as if he was the visitor. "Annie tells me she ran away from home. That the bruises on her face are from her father."

"That's why I took her in."

"You should have notified us."

"Who did?"

"Reports are confidential."

"A minister keeps confidences. I would have contacted you, if she were still in danger."

"She's a child. Pregnant, as I assume you know. At risk," she said, tapping her pencil on a manila folder.

He half expected her to reach into her brief case to draw out a ruler and slap his knuckles. Perhaps distrusting men was an occupational hazard, in her line of work.

"She should have seen a doctor," she said reproachfully.

"I've offered."

"We will arrange that, and counseling regarding the baby."

"If she decides on adoption, I know a family."

"Placement is not for you to decide. For now, there's the Crittendon Home in Pittsburgh for unwed mothers."

"She's welcome here."

"You are not approved to foster. She should be with a woman. She may stay tonight, while I make arrangements at the Crit. I'll see you in the morning."

He found Annie in the rocking chair across from the shop counter.

"She said I have to go to a place in Pittsburgh. She says I have to see a doctor."

"She's right about the doctor."

The rest of the day passed like hours in a departure lounge, waiting to say goodbye. He did not open the shop, working instead on the cradle. The distressed grain of the wood, the delicate pattern of wormholes, pleased him. Annie sat on a stool close by. He kept the door open to disperse the fumes—dangerous for the baby.

After supper they walked to the Little League game, returning in the dark. He scooped ice cream. They ate out back, while the moon rose. Its silver light cast no shadow on his sundial's injunction to count only the sunny hours. The mint breathed out a faint fragrance.

"Good night," she said, scraping her spoon against the empty bowl, licking it.

"More?" he said. There it was again, the twinge, the sharp ache in his chest.

"No, thank you. Thank you for everything."

"You're more than welcome, Annie."

"I don't want to go to that place. I wish I could stay."

"If it were up to me, you would. We'll work it out my dear, my home is your home."

He sat alone for a spell by the light of the cool moon and the distant stars, with the bats flitting above, before walking to the garage. The door groaned as it slid up the tracks, breaking the stillness. At the workbench he rocked the cradle back and forth and picked up his sandpaper. He worked until he was too tired to do anything but go to bed.

Morning came. He knocked on Annie's door. The social worker would come soon; he wanted their last breakfast alone together.

"Annie, breakfast time."

No answer.

"Time to rise and shine,"

No answer. He opened the door.

The sofa bed was folded away, linens and pillows in a neat pile. The closet was empty, the bureau bare. He hurried into the shop, heart skipping and banging. The cash register was open. There had only been about fifty dollars. If he had known, if he had thought, he would have left more.

He waited on the church steps. His neighbor watered her tomatoes as though he were invisible. The social worker arrived.

"She's ready?"

"Gone."

"What do you mean?"

"When I woke up this morning she was gone."

"Girls like her are just bent on disaster. Sometimes I wonder why we try to save them."

Salvation is not in your hands, he thought.

"If you hear from her, or learn her whereabouts, call. She needs to see a doctor."

The neighbor's screen door slammed.

He retreated into the dark garage and stood at the workbench, rocking the empty cradle back and forth.

Known by Heart

Alan was accustomed to Grace's carelessness. She always left behind a
wake of mislaid eyeglasses and car keys, overdue library books, socks
without mates.

"You should be more careful," he told her. "Slow down, pay
attention."

She seemed to court chaos and close calls. Years earlier she had a
fender-bender on her way to work. She admitted afterward how fright-
ening it had been to feel warm blood dripping down her face, seeping
into her mouth. "Then I tasted coffee!" She laughed and did not give
up balancing the mug on her lap as she drove. He had been torn between
relief she was not hurt and irritation at her slap dash habits.

She was not careless of people, remembering birthdays and anniver-
saries and standing first in line with casseroles and comfort after death
and divorce. And he paid close enough attention to things for them
both. What he noticed and she forgot, what she attended to and he
neglected, had become part of the complementary distribution of labor
in their long partnership.

The beginning was subtle, like a message slipped under the door.
She left the plug in the laundry tub and ran the washer and the basement
flooded. The gas tank was empty every time he got in her car. Then it
was the bills.

"I wrote the check, I did, I'm sure," she said.

"Then what did you do with it?"

"I mailed it, of course. Why wouldn't I mail it?" She was rattled.

"You're retired, you have less to do, and you're doing less," he said,
taking over the checkbook.

Their daughter Frances lived nearby. Grace often took one of their twin granddaughters to the playground, giving Frances one-on-one time with the other. Alan was in his office at the University when the call came from a borrowed cell phone.

"I can't find her. I can't find the baby."

He jumped in the car and sped the two miles to the park. It was the first warm day of spring, the sandbox overflowed with children, the slides swarmed. Even so, it was easy to pick out his little granddaughter, stolid and quiet, digging in the cold, damp sand with the delight and absorption he remembered on Frances's face thirty years before.

"Grace, she's right there, under your nose."

"Oh, my goodness, so she is. I forgot what she was wearing. I was so frightened I couldn't see her."

Alan sat shivering in the thin spring sunshine; he had not even taken time to put on his raincoat as he scrambled out the office door. He realized there was also something he had not seen, right under his nose.

The next steps, the tests, the diagnosis, were formalities. He sat with her in the neurologist's office.

"Today's date?" She smiled at the doctor, her charming smile. "Heavens, isn't that silly... I'm retired you know. The days just run together." She turned to Alan, "Dear, what is the date?"

"He's asking you."

Frances came with them to the appointment after the testing was finished. Alan distrusted the luxury of the doctor's office, the leather couch, the oriental rug: comfort meant to soften the blow of bad news. He sat beside Grace, holding her hand. The doctor confirmed what Alan already knew. Grace flinched when she heard the word. She did not cry until they were home and called their younger daughter Kate in Chicago.

He doled out the medicine the doctor had been careful to explain could only "slow the progress, not reverse it or halt it." It was the only medicine she took except for vitamins and antibiotics before the dentist cleaned her teeth, a precaution due to a residual heart murmur from childhood rheumatic fever. "The antibiotic protects against infective endocarditis," the dentist said. Alan had looked up infective endocarditis in his *Merck Manual*: "Untreated infective endocarditis is always fatal. Physicians recommend anti-microbial prophylaxis for high risk patients during oral-dental procedures."

He taught his last class at the University and retired, sooner than he had intended. Alan tried to do as the neurologist said, "Put a safety net around her, but let her do as much as she can within it." When she could not find her way home from the grocery store, he hid her car keys and scolded her for losing them again. He gave her car to Frances.

Grace protested. "You are being ridiculous, I'm not some teenager. I have been driving fifty years." Better she be angry with him than cause an accident, better to be angry with him than realize what was happening.

He missed everything about teaching, even faculty meetings. His days were full and tedious—cooking, laundry, shopping. One day he returned from the grocery store and found Grace kneeling in the study, surrounded by piles of books. The shelves were bare. She'd worked in a second-hand book store for a time and collected poetry, specializing in first editions of modern American poets. Although a casual housekeeper, she kept her books in alphabetical order.

"Someone's been in my books," she said.

He knelt in the rubble and began to make piles by author. She wandered out of the room.

Grace began to mix up night and day. He would awaken and find her side of the bed cold. Pulling on a robe he would stumble downstairs and discover her yanking books from the shelves in frantic search for what had been taken from her.

"We're seeing the progression from mild to moderate," the neurologist said. "Try day care. Her social skills are intact."

Only someone who had not known her could say her social skills were intact. Alan remembered the laughing blond girl she had been, the most popular girl on campus, president of her sorority. *The way to have a friend is to be a friend. If you don't know what to say to someone, ask questions. Take an interest,* she had taught their daughters.

"Get an alarm system and identification bracelets. She won't remember her address and phone, if she's lost," the doctor continued.

"She never leaves the house without me."

"Just in case."

They drove past the zoo on their way home from the doctor's and he pulled in. It was a golden, warm Indian summer day. The sort of day made precious by the threat of winter.

"Oh, how lovely. The zoo," she said.

They walked together, holding hands, up and down the hilly, winding paths. He looked for the little golden tamarind monkeys in the trees, an endangered species. The zoo let them roam free, tracking them with tiny radio transmitters, hardening monkeys born and bred in captivity to be released in the South American jungle. Inside the monkey house he contemplated pairs of small gray monkeys, tails entwined. What if one fell? Did the other lose its balance?

They ate dinner on the way home. She took so long coming back to the table from the bathroom he asked the waitress to check. In a few minutes Grace crossed the dining room clutching the waitress's hand.

"She got stuck in the stall," said the waitress.

"The door was broken," said Grace.

He ordered the identification bracelets, his and hers, caretaker and care recipient. But when the bracelets arrived, he did not use them. Instead he taped one of their address labels to the sterling bracelet she had sent to him at boot camp, inscribed with his name, rank, serial number, and *Your Grace* engraved on the back.

"Wear this, dear," he said, slipping the bracelet on her wrist.

"Thank you. How pretty."

He did not install an alarm system or enroll her in day care.

"I won't turn our home into a fortress, or send her off to some warehouse," he told Kate when she called from Chicago, alerted by her sister.

Grace was quiet when they went to dinner with old friends; the conversation streamed past her. She seemed to take her cues from him, laughing politely only after he did. Her gracious habits persisted: "How are you? Lovely to see you." The words were like rote dialogue memorized in foreign language class; she could not improvise. Fewer invitations came and Alan stopped accepting most. She was restless at movies and concerts, and he was anxious if she had to use the restroom. He tried slide shows.

"Look, darling, there you are when Kate was born." Alan fed slides into the magic lantern: Grace, blond hair frizzy with heat, pulling aphids from her prize pink roses; running behind Frances, balancing the girl's little two-wheeled bicycle; laughing over her shoulder as she leaned into her stroke in the canoe. He stared at the screen, devouring the images. Grace was oblivious, dozing in her chair. Alan turned off the projector and helped her up to bed.

One night he awoke to the insistent buzz of the smoke alarm. She was not beside him. He stumbled downstairs to the kitchen. Grace stood at the stove over a blazing skillet; he pushed her aside and sprayed the fire extinguisher.

"What in god's name were you doing? Stay out of the kitchen," he said, shoving her into the dining room.

She looked at him with a mixture of defiance and fright. He recalled the same expression on Kate's face when she was three and he discovered her on the carpet in a puddle of her own urine. Alan glimpsed his face, flushed with anger, in the mirror over the sideboard.

"I'm sorry, dear," he said, unable to tell if her bland gaze constituted forgiveness or just forgetfulness.

After the kitchen fire, Frances insisted he hire someone.

"You both are losing weight, Daddy. You look exhausted, you must get some help."

"We have help."

"A cleaning lady! Who comes, what, once every two weeks? That's not what I'm talking about."

Frances called an agency and Wanda invaded the spare room with her fragrant hair pomades and heavy wheeled suitcases.

"Who's that woman?" Grace asked him every day. "There's a strange woman here."

"Wanda. She's helping."

"We don't need help. I don't want her touching my things."

Though Grace was frightened of bathing and confused by dressing, Wanda could coax her into the tub and ease her into the baffling bras and slips. Alan thought of how gentle but effective Grace had been with their little daughters. Why were women better with this sort of thing? Wanda watched him, judging him, when he became impatient.

Wanda was a night owl. After Alan and Grace went to bed, she cooked spicy stews for the next day, talked on the phone, played island music on the radio. One night Grace's screams awoke Alan.

"Get out, get out! Help! Police!"

He ran downstairs and found the two women in the kitchen, glaring at each other.

"This woman has broken in," Grace said.

Alan let Wanda go the next day, two weeks' severance pay in lieu of notice. "It just wasn't working out," he told his daughters.

They always closed their weekend farm on Columbus Day. That summer they had only used the place once. Grace had been ill at ease away from home and Alan had not tried again. The girls, busy with their lives, did not come. For years he had paid the closest neighbor to mow the lawn and keep the meadow behind the house open. Most of the old fields were grown over now, the woods crept closer to the house every year, like tide up a beach. He knew he should think about selling. But whether they kept or sold the place, the water had to be turned off for the winter. Columbus Day weekend Alan and Grace drove out of the city toward the farm, leaving early before the holiday rush hour traffic. As they drove toward the turnpike, she kept looking over her shoulder into the empty back seat.

"We've left the children. We must go back for the girls," she said.

"We haven't forgotten anyone. They are grown; Frances has children of her own."

"We've left the children. We must go back for the girls," she repeated every few miles.

He did not bother to reply. After a time, she closed her eyes and seemed to sleep.

When she awoke, she was calmer and made no mention of the children. The sun was setting; the western sky blazed gold as if in competition with the brilliant leaves.

"What beautiful light," she said. And then out of nowhere, as if some blocked channel had momentarily opened, she recited a line of poetry he recognized, "It will flame out, like shining from shook foil." She closed her eyes again.

He drove up the steep hill and stopped in front of the farmhouse. "Here we are," Alan said, turning off the engine.

He led her onto the porch. Gazing out over the meadow framed with bright foliage she looked sad. He was grateful for the frank emotion rather than the impassive mask her face was becoming. Alan put his arm around her; the last rays of sunset gilded the trees.

Her quiet mood evaporated. Evening was her worst time; she was tired and fractious. She seemed uneasy, as though the farmhouse were unfamiliar. Grace paced back and forth from the parlor to the kitchen as he boiled water for spaghetti and heated the frozen sauce Grace had made. How many summers ago? The label in her neat block letters read *Marinara, August 14*. He remembered the kitchen filled with steam and the fragrance of tomatoes and herbs as she chopped and hummed and stirred.

"Where are the children? Did we leave the children in the car?"

He opened the wine and poured himself a glass. "Do you want some wine?" he asked.

She left the room but was back again in a moment. "Did we leave the children in the car?"

The wine, the fatigue of the drive and the day, overcame him. "Stop it! Sit down and be quiet!" he shouted.

"It doesn't hurt to be nice," she said, as she used to say to the girls when they quarreled with each other or sassed her. But she did sit down in the hickory rocking chair by the window. She rocked back and forth and did not speak again.

Repentant, he lit candles for dinner, and poured her a generous goblet of wine, hoping it would help her sleep. She slumped over her plate and did not finish her pasta. He helped her up the steep stairs to their bedroom. He opened the bag he had packed for her and took out the nightgown.

"Arms up." Alan pulled the soft old gown over her rounded shoulders, her shrunken sagging breasts. He tucked her in and kissed her forehead.

"Thank you, dear," she said.

He gazed out the wavery antique glass of the window. They used to lie in bed and watch the moon rise through this window, making love bathed in silver light, no need for curtains in the country. She fell asleep; he left the room and went downstairs.

He washed the dishes. The china pattern was a winter scene, a barn and trees. She sparkled with excitement, bidding for these dishes at a country auction and carried them home like trophies from a race.

Grace whimpered as he eased into bed, but the wine had done its work and she did not wake. He watched the moon cross the sky as he fell asleep.

It was dark when he woke; the moon was gone from the window. The sheets beside him were cold and empty. He tripped down the narrow stairs. The front door gaped open and night air blew into the room. He ran into the yard.

"Grace, Grace!" he called into the vast blackness of the country night. She was swallowed up in the dark. He went back into the house for a flashlight and swung it back and forth, like the beacon of a feeble lighthouse, bellowing her name until his throat was raw.

He telephoned the nearest neighbors.

"Sorry to bother you, but Grace has wandered off." His voice broke.

"We'll be right there."

Bill and Mary arrived in their pick-up, the deer-spotting searchlight sweeping along the roadside ditch and into the deep shadows of the woods.

"How long has she been gone?"

"I woke up and she wasn't there."

"Get a coat and shoes, Alan," said Mary gently. Like a mother.

But if he was cold what about Grace, wherever she was? He should stay as he was; suffer with her.

"Go get something warm on," Mary insisted.

"Turn on all the lights in the house," said Bill. "And ring that dinner bell on the porch. I'll take the south side of the hill, toward the spring. Mary, go down the north side. Alan, you stay here in case she comes back. Keep ringing the bell."

They pulled flashlights and guns out of the truck.

"We'll fire a shot when we find her. If we're not back in half an hour, if you don't hear a gun go off, call the fire department to come up and help," said Bill.

It was a relief to be given instructions. And a relief to hear Bill say *when we find her.* Alan pulled on his old army jacket and laced up his boots. He rang the dinner bell on the porch. Grace had bought the huge bell at the hardware store so she could summon the girls to dinner from secret forest forts, rambles by the stream. Now he called out to Grace with her bell. The flashlight beam flickered down the meadow until Bill disappeared in the woods. Alan's arm grew tired; he switched to the other. Both arms and shoulders burned. Thirty minutes passed. No gunshot, no flashlight glimmering back up the meadow. He should call the fire department.

Once years before at the beach, Alan and Grace dozed off in the sun with the little girls digging at their feet and awoke to find Frances digging alone, Kate vanished. He remembered the frenzied jog up the beach, young lifeguards jolted into action. They found her, digging nearby with another child. He remembered the relief of having Kate, warm and damp and gritty, back in his arms. And he remembered the shame of their public lapse in parental vigilance.

He went inside, dialed.

"Fire and Rescue," answered a sleepy voice. The Fire Department was all volunteer here in the country.

"Alan Murray. From the ridge road, the old Carr place. My wife Grace has dementia; she's wandered off. We can't find her."

"O.K. Hold on. We'll be there."

Back on the porch Alan resumed ringing the bell, throwing his whole weight and strength into it, as if determination would bring her out of the shadows, as if he were Orpheus playing the lyre to lure Eurydice back from Hades.

The fire truck and ambulance rumbled up the hill, lights blazing and sirens blaring. Alarms were common in the city, but here the sirens split the quiet of the country night like a scream.

A young fireman came up on the porch. Alan thought he recognized him. His father ran the hardware store and serviced their furnace. It was embarrassing, needing help up here. The responders were not an anonymous crew like in the city.

"How long she been gone?"

"I don't know. I woke up about an hour ago and she wasn't in bed. My neighbors are in the woods, looking."

"What was she wearing?"

"A nightgown, I don't know if she even has her slippers."

The man clumped down the porch steps. He spoke to the huddle of men and they dispersed, along the road, down into the forest.

Alan wanted to go along but he was marooned on deck while others dove in the sea of the dark forest, trolling for Grace. He rang the bell. It was all he could do.

Then he saw a young man walking up the hill, carrying something like a load of crumpled laundry in his arms. Alan almost fell down the steps in his haste.

"She's conscious," said the man. His partner ran ahead and turned on the truck siren and his neighbors and the other men appeared from the woods like shadows. They brought a stretcher from the ambulance; laid her on it, with surprising tenderness for such bulky men and lifted the gurney into the ambulance.

"You can ride along in back."

A man in the ambulance reached down and pulled him up. Inside he saw they had already cut her wet nightgown off. She lay still as a corpse, eyes closed. He shut his eyes a moment, too, and when he looked again she was buried under blankets. The ambulance was cold, and the seat was hard. They sped through the night.

"We're admitting her. To warm her, hydrate her. And for observation, since she has that heart murmur, a cold heart can be prone to problems," the doctor at the county hospital said.

She doesn't have a cold heart, Alan wanted to say. *That has never been her problem.* He called Frances from the lobby phone while Grace lay in Emergency, waiting for a room.

"Oh, Daddy. You should never have gone up there by yourself. This is it. She's too much for you."

"Not now. Call your sister. I'll talk to you tomorrow."

He spent the night at her bedside, in a plastic reclining chair. The nurse brought him blankets and a pillow. Grace stirred and moaned when the nurse took her vitals, but she did not open her eyes. He dreamed he was back again in the forest of the Ardennes, trapped with his patrol behind enemy lines, in the cold and in danger.

In the morning she opened her eyes and stared around the room. She looked at him, face rigid and blank.

"It's O.K. I'm right here," he said.

There was no glimmer of recognition.

"It's not uncommon, after a trauma, in an unfamiliar place, for someone with her condition to lose ground, be more confused, for a time. Her vitals are fine. She's stable; you can take her home today," the doctor said.

Frances arrived; she must have driven the two hours from the city as soon as it was light. She hurried to the bedside.

"Mother, how are you?"

Grace closed her eyes as though the question were too difficult to answer.

"Kate and I want you to find a place where she'll be safe, and well cared for," Frances whispered.

"She's safe and well cared for with me," he said. And remembered his failure had brought them here to the hospital.

"We were lucky this time, Daddy. What if it happened at home? She could be hit by a car in the dark."

"It wouldn't happen there. She was upset by being away from home."

He put his head in his hands. Frances drew her chair closer and stroked his shoulder.

"I need the bathroom," Grace said. The first words she had spoken since the nightmare began. "Young lady," she said, looking at Frances, "Where's the bathroom?"

Alan took her home, refusing the doctor's recommendations and his daughters' entreaties that he hire help. As the doctor had predicted, her confusion cleared a little. She knew him, and seemed to know the girls, but never used their names again, calling them "Dear" instead. She was clever at hiding what she had lost, beneath a bright tone and vacuous smile.

He did not attend the caregiver support group Frances found for him. He was too busy and besides, what was the point of hearing that worse was coming? He did have an alarm system installed but tried to never leave her alone. Frances brought her girls and came to stay while he ran errands.

"Where have you been? Out with Ivy?" Grace always asked when he returned.

There had been the one affair, years back. Afterward, they repaired the damage and went on. She had forgotten so much; why did she remember that?

Frances set up an appointment for him to visit Sylvan Woods Assisted Living. She came to stay with Grace.

"Just go visit, Daddy. The dementia unit there has a good reputation."

The marketing director met him in the lobby. She wore a blue suit that blended in like camouflage with the teal and mauve upholstery and drapes. Perhaps it was a required uniform, like an airline stewardess. The door to the dementia unit was painted with a bright mural. It took him a moment to recognize Oz, the Emerald City.

She tapped on the keypad. "It's a locked unit of course, the code is our zip; they don't know it."

A gas fire burned in the first room, an eternal facsimile flame flickering in a plaster fireplace glued to the wall like a piece of scenery.

"Isn't it cozy? We use a modified Eden approach, state of the art. Notice our kitty, and all the plants."

A few women slumped in chairs. One held the cat, another a limp half-dressed baby doll. As his guide ushered him further down the hall, the pretense of hotel faded into something more institutional.

"Here's the lounge," she said. "Right by the nurse's station. All the residents' corridors lead here. This is where the action is. They all love it."

It was not a room, just a broad lobby. A trompe l'oeil mural of a front porch, complete with flower boxes and wicker furniture, stretched across one wall; a large television hung on another. Frail bodies sat swallowed up in high-backed chairs, oblivious to the jaunty sailors singing and tapping across the television screen in a black and white movie. A gray-haired woman in a long green housecoat shuffled up and grabbed his wrist.

"Good to see you, dear," she said.

He pulled away, ashamed of his eagerness to escape.

"And here's our dining room. Just four to a table. The residents can come in between meals, too. We keep spoons and napkins and some plastic dishes in the cupboard. They like to set the table."

Alan remembered the Montessori nursery school his daughters had attended. Frances had insisted they set the table at home exactly the way she learned in class. He and Grace laughed over their bossy little girl, so sure she knew what was right, what was best for them.

A tiny woman in a wheel chair was parked by one of the tables, shredding a pile of paper napkins with fierce concentration. The director whisked Alan down the hall.

"This is our activity room. Busy, busy, all the time. A girl scout troop is coming to do manicures this afternoon. They love to have their nails done."

Alan did not believe Grace had ever had her nails done. Their daughters had collected scores of bottles of nail varnish, dozens of tubes of lipstick, during their teen years. He and Grace had been amused by the girls' claim on feminine territory that had never interested their mother, a harmless rebellion Grace called it.

"Let me show you a resident's room," the director said. "You see, we have the family bring in a photo to put on the door, it helps the resident know where home is. The rooms are doubles of course, toilet and sink *en suite*. We shower them down the hall. We encourage family to bring special personal items, so long as nothing's valuable. See how cozy this room is."

The hand knit blanket, the old rocking chair, looked out of place, inadequate garnish in the anonymous room.

"And then of course we have our garden. Safe and secure, with lovely serpentine paths. Would you like to see?"

"Not today. I should be getting back home."

He fled to the parking lot and leaned against the car, gulping down the fresh air.

Alan found his wife and daughter in the living room. Grace was turning pages in a book, fast and automatic as though shuffling a deck of cards. She no longer read, but seemed to like the feel of a book in her hands. He dropped a kiss on her hair.

"Where have you been? With Ivy?" she asked.

"Errands."

In the kitchen Frances put on her coat and picked up her car keys.

"What did you think?"

"It's a mausoleum."

"Daddy, don't. You're worn out. We've got to do something. You can't keep this up."

He stood at the kitchen counter preparing chicken breasts for dinner. A postcard had come last week from the dentist, a picture of a tooth with a string around it. Her appointment was tomorrow. He had propped the card in the kitchen windowsill to make sure he remembered. Perhaps Grace's condition was contagious, he was forgetting more now, too.

Don't forget, time for your check up! the card said. The receptionist had added a note, *Doctor says to call if you need a refill on Grace's antibiotic.* He had checked the medicine cabinet the day the card arrived; the orange plastic vial of amoxicillin was still half full.

"Delicious," she said, though he'd grilled the chicken too long and it tasted tough and dry.

He helped Grace get ready for bed; stood beside her in the bathroom while she brushed her teeth.

"Brush well, we have the dentist tomorrow."

Alan tucked her in, retrieved the bottle of antibiotic from the medicine cabinet and took it downstairs, leaving it on the kitchen windowsill beside the dentist's reminder card.

His attention wandered from the newspaper. The biography of General Grant was too heavy to even hold so late at night. He worried his concentration was waning. Was he losing interest in the world like Grace had?

Once in bed, Alan fell asleep but not into a deep slumber, just a tense dozing. He awoke in the middle of the night; her side of the bed was empty. He hurried downstairs. Grace knelt on the study floor, rifling through a book, ripping out pages. He coaxed her back to bed and went downstairs to repair the damage.

Alan smoothed a crumpled page. *The art of losing isn't hard to master.* Elizabeth Bishop.

He was too tired to continue cleaning up, too tired to sleep. He poured some scotch and sat looking into the empty hearth. They used to enjoy eating supper on the coffee table in front of the open fire; he did not dare light fires now. What might she do, alone down here in the middle of the night, hot embers smoldering? He finished his drink and went to the kitchen and put the glass in the dishwasher.

Alan took the vial of pills from the windowsill and stood shaking it back and forth. He walked into the bathroom and stood above the toilet, rattling the capsules in the bottle. It would be so easy to dump them. Easy to flush the intended prophylaxis away.

Alan replaced the bottle on the window sill.

He went up to bed. It would be morning soon.

Estates and Trust

The memorial service was a mistake. Her sister Frances had made the arrangements before Kate arrived. Heinz Chapel was too large for the handful of her father's elderly friends and former colleagues. Afterward, at the Faculty Club, the gray-haired guests nibbled dry sandwiches and sipped lukewarm tea. Kate looked around the room. This was the last time she would see these people. She would never be a child in anyone's eyes again.

The sisters dismantled his apartment in the retirement home the next day. There was so little, it felt more like a hotel suite than a home. Kate wept unexpected tears over the drawer of undershirts, worn and washed often, frayed souvenirs of his thrift. *Turn the light out if you are leaving the room* had been the refrain of her childhood. Now, she switched on every light in the apartment but it did not dispel the chill gloom. In the kitchen the white dishes went in a box for Goodwill. The cookie jar, a squat ceramic house, sat beside the refrigerator, as it had in her childhood home. She lifted the blue roof (cracked and mended since she dropped it years ago reaching in for a cookie after school) and pulled out a handful of stale animal crackers. The refrigerator was empty, except for a Styrofoam box of leftovers from the dining room downstairs and his usual bottle of dry sherry.

Kate filled two tumblers with sherry and brought one to Frances who knelt in a pool of papers beside the desk. Kate noticed the gray roots of her sister's hair. She must have stopped coloring it. Frances was forty-six, just a year older than Kate. Yesterday at the memorial service when someone said, "Kate, you look so young, just like your mother always did," she had felt Frances stiffen beside her. Her sister had always resented Kate's resemblance to their mother. Frances had been adopted after their parents had tried and failed for years to have a child. Soon afterward the couple conceived. So, Frances turned one just as Kate was born. Frances had been keeping track of injustices ever since. *Life isn't fair, sweetie,* their mother used to say, coaxing Frances out of a mood. Kate missed her mother, gone a dozen years.

"What should we do with all these letters?" Frances asked, rocking back on her haunches and taking a deep sip of sherry.

"Didn't he give all his papers to the University when he moved here?"

"These are personal. To Mother during the war, it looks like."

"Keep them in the attic," Kate said.

Frances had a big attic. After their mother died, Frances and her then husband had bought the house the girls had grown up in. Kate had not expected her father to sell and move away from Schenley Park and the university. But he had seemed almost eager to leave the house, as though he could leave the memories of the hard, recent years behind. He sold it to Frances for much less than it was worth, pleased to keep the house in the family. During her recent divorce, Frances had managed to hold onto it.

"I may have to move. I can't keep everything."

"Okay, I'll take the cookie jar," Kate said.

"You don't eat cookies. I want it for the girls." Frances had deep circles beneath her eyes.

"But you have mother's dishes." *Don't squabble,* she heard her mother's voice.

Frances's house had been full of the noisy combustion of family life until last year. Her twin daughters left for college and her husband for his graduate student. The house was still full of things Kate coveted: their mother's photograph albums, her cedar chest, the Chippendale dining table, the Haviland china. But Kate had no space for things in Chicago, in the one-bedroom Hyde Park apartment she had intended to be temporary when she started working at the university twenty years earlier.

"Take his letters to the attic at the farm then," Kate said.

"The farm? I can't look after it, too. You've barely been there in years. We're not keeping a vacation place as a museum, or using it as a storage locker. We'll sell it."

Everything shook loose inside Kate, as it had last week when she heard Frances's voice on her answering machine. *He died this morning. Call me.*

She had tried but failed to retrieve her father's last message to her, from several days earlier.

"Sell the farm?"

"I have my hands full taking care of one old house. I'm done with taking care of everything for everyone." Frances's nose turned pink. She went into the bathroom and shut the door. Kate heard the water running to cover crying.

She put the contested cookie jar in a carton, packed the letters around it, sealed the top, and marked it *Kate/Letters*. Father would not approve of her sneaking. Integrity, in matters big and small, had been his hallmark. But she was tired and there was not time to negotiate over everything. They had to be out of his apartment by the end of the day. At least they agreed the shabby furniture would be donated; anything good or comfortable was already at Frances's or the farm.

The sisters shut the door to the apartment for the final time. Kate drove her father's car to the house. She wanted to drive straight on two hours to the farm and barricade herself inside the way she used to slam her bedroom door and lock it when she and Frances fought. Once the key jammed and Kate was trapped inside. Sweaty and crying, she'd heard rapping at the window. Her father's square-jawed, freckled face smiled in. Never an athlete, he'd climbed a tall ladder like a fireman to the rescue. Both girls' keys disappeared after that. *If a door is closed, respect each other's privacy,* said their mother.

For dinner, Frances made grilled cheese. Kate preferred salads and sushi but tonight the rich comfort food of their childhood tasted wonderful. Frances had put on weight since Christmas, since the divorce became final, during their father's final weeks. Kate herself was shriveling up.

"Have you been dieting?" Frances had asked right away as they waited at the baggage claim.

"No. Swimming."

Really, she was losing weight because of eating regular healthy meals at regular healthy hours instead of delicious snacks at odd moments with her lover when he stole away from his family. He was on sabbatical in Milan with his wife. For years Frances had warned, *You're wasting your time waiting for him.* Now that Frances herself had been left, the sisters did not discuss Kate's situation.

They ate on their parents' rickety TV trays and watched the news in the room she still thought of as her father's study. It was strange to see Frances sitting in his chair. Were his sunflower seed husks lodged between the cushions? The news ended.

"So tomorrow we have to go out to Bedford to the attorney. Typical having his affairs handled near the farm where it's cheaper," said Frances.

"Generous with the big things. College. Letting you have the house."

"I paid for the house, and I'm still paying! I don't have time to spend all day going out and back to see some country lawyer. I've used up all my leave on Daddy."

Kate heard the unspoken reproach. *Where were you when we needed you?*

"Well, I'll stay at the farm a few days and then drive on to Chicago." Kate was keeping his car. All these years and she had never had one. She was an orphan and a grown up now.

"Better hope the furnace is working. He didn't get out there last fall."

"There's the wood stove."

Frances left the room.

Sitting in her father's chair, Kate slipped a hand down the gritty crevice between the upholstered arm and seat cushion and found the smooth hard husks of sunflower seeds. She went to the kitchen, poured a glass of his sherry from the apartment, and perused the refrigerator door, busy with photographs, newspaper clippings, lists, appointment cards. The once cheerful litter was history now.

Kate had only sparse lines of magnetic poetry on her own narrow refrigerator. Sometimes her lover played with them. She studied the words after he left, trying to find a declaration, a promise in the random phrases stuck to her freezer door.

Awakening early, she left Frances a note. *Meet you at the lawyer's.* Kate took Route 30, the Lincoln Highway, to Bedford instead of the turnpike. The clock at the corner by the bank was gone, otherwise the quiet streets of gray stone buildings were unchanged since her last visit, six or seven years back. She drove past the fairgrounds, past the Come Clean Launderette, to the diner shaped like a giant coffee pot. The silver paint was peeling off the pot's tarpaper sides.

"Coffee to go, please. And a muffin."

"Doughnut okay?"

Always doughnuts here. She and Frances devoured doughnuts their first summer at the farm when she was ten, teasing each about becoming plump like the women on the lake beach in baggy bathing suits, a hilarious and impossible fate.

She drove on toward the village, spotting the red roof of the Methodist church belfry. Last week, browsing through a Chicago bookshop, dazed with grief, passing time until she flew east, she had picked up a glossy guidebook for Pennsylvania and found a photograph of this familiar square belfry. It was like discovering a local girl in a fashion magazine. Her reflex had been to buy the book for her father; he had taken such a proprietary interest in this region.

The road wound through the village and up the steep ridge to the farm. Early in March no leaves obscured the bare bones of the Alleghenies. The walnut tree still stood sentinel out front, but the massive bough where their swing had hung was gone, struck by lightning. The tree looked unbalanced, like an amputee. On the porch she looked out across the valley at the distant ridges. The view her father loved would be eternal, whatever happened to the farm. Or would it? There'd been talk of fracking. And wasn't that a windmill?

Inside, it was dim. Her father always left the curtains drawn as a security measure. The room was cold as the mortuary where she had last seen him. She opened the frayed muslin curtains her mother had made on her Singer Featherweight. The room was the same: braided rugs on scuffed pine floors, oak dining table with clawed feet, hickory rocking chairs, locally made. Hard to believe her parents were gone forever, not just away.

His typed instructions for turning on the furnace and the water hung on the hook at the bottom of the cellar stairs. Her mother had lovingly scoffed about the degree of pedantic detail. But now it was comforting to have him tell her what to do. She flipped the furnace switch and it shuddered on; she closed all the valves on the tangle of pipes across the ceiling and turned on the pump. Kneeling by the water tank she held the little lever at the precise forty-five-degree angle he prescribed.

Oh, no! An unexpected cascade of water was splashing somewhere in the cellar. Kate turned off the pump and went to investigate.

The dirt floor in the former coal room was already wet, the thin copper pipe above had split. Her father must not have drained the water properly the last time he was here. The pipe had frozen and burst.

Someone was knocking on the door upstairs. Knees stiff with cold, she climbed out of the cellar. Bill stood on the porch though for just a moment she thought it was the other Bill, his father. But the older man had been gone for years now. Her parents had gone to the funeral. Her mother had still been well enough to tell her about it.

"Saw the car. We heard about your dad. Stopped to tell you I'm sorry."

"Thanks." *We heard.* He was married now.

"You look the same, Katy."

"Hardly. I'd recognize you, though." She was blushing, like a kid.

"You get the heat and the water on O.K.?"

"A pipe's burst. I was just going to call the hardware store."

"Mind if I look? I helped your dad the last time this happened."

He headed down the cellar stairs; she followed.

She smelled outdoor air and the musk of barn animals as they stood inches apart in the cold cellar. They had not been so close, or so alone, in thirty years.

"Could have been worse. This section's easy to get to." He reached up and put his hand on the pipe above her head. She remembered that hand. Kate led the way upstairs, conscious of him close behind her.

"I'll bring my soldering gear and pick up some pipe. Fix it up for you after school."

"School?"

"High school. I teach biology. Takes more than moonlighting to keep a farm these days."

"No, I'll just call down to the hardware. They'll send someone."

"I'd like to do it."

His gaze was candid and kind. *Accept graciously,* her mother used to say. If she did, he'd be back.

"Thanks. Frances is coming. We have to go into town later today, see the attorney."

"Okay if I let myself in if you're not back? We still have the key, been keeping an eye on the place for your dad. My son does the mowing."

"How old is he?"

"Seventeen. Call Susan, if you need to use the commode down at our place."

"There's the outhouse. And I can get water from the village." An artesian spring bubbled up from the core of the earth into a trough in front of the general store; her father bottled the water and brought it back to Pittsburgh.

"See you later." He ducked outside, climbed into his pickup and drove away.

Kate wanted tea and opened the china cupboard for the pot before remembering—no water. She lifted out a plate, remembering her mother bringing the set home from an auction. *Friendly Village,* the pattern was called, a winter scene in the country, a day almost like today: late winter or early spring, brown and gray and the barn's red.

At the window she gazed through the rippled glass at what had been her mother's garden. Gone, and the field beyond overgrown by shoots of maple and black walnut saplings. But she made out the deer blind at the edge of the woods.

Bill's father had had permission to hunt their land, plant their fields and use the hay, in exchange for mowing around the house, keeping an eye on the place. He built the tree stand: during hunting season it was off limits to the children. But in those early summers, it was their camouflaged tree fort, a stage for re-enacting the French and Indian War and the siege of Fort Bedford. Bill, a year older than Frances, two years older than Kate, joined the sisters when he finished his morning chores, and played all day until he went home to do chores again. The girls argued over who would sit beside him at lunch until their mother said, *one more word and I send him home. I will sit next to Bill.* Frances and Kate would smile across at him while kicking each other beneath the table. After Bill turned thirteen, he no longer came to play—farming all through the long summer days with his father. The girls only saw him when he came to mow the lawn or help his father cut the hay in the fields near their house.

One afternoon, the summer Kate was fourteen, she stayed behind when her mother and Frances went grocery shopping in town. Her father pecked on his typewriter upstairs; she sat on the porch swing reading *Gone with the Wind.* Bill came to mow. Peering over the edge of her book, she watched him work, his bare back gleaming with sweat. He finished and came onto the porch, shrugging into a plaid cotton shirt.

"Would you like some lemonade?" Her mother never let any guest go thirsty.

"Sure," he said.

All summer her mother kept a glass pitcher full of homemade lemonade: sweet artesian water and thin slices of lemon, sprigs of garden mint, only a little sugar. Kate filled two heavy glass tumblers. She sat beside him on the porch swing, breathing the mingled scent of fresh cut grass and sweat. The swing creaked, cicadas and crickets droned. His arm slipped around her shoulders, his fingers pressed the bare flesh of her upper arm. He kissed her, just barely grazing her lips. His own were cool and bittersweet from lemonade. But the kiss was interrupted by the sound of the car out front.

Bill walked to the porch steps and almost collided with Kate's mother as she climbed up, a bag of groceries in her arms.

"Can I help you with that?"

"Thank you. And for cutting the grass. It smells so good. Care to stay for a glass of lemonade?"

"No, thanks. Kate gave me one."

After he was gone, Kate saw her sister stare at the two glasses close together on the porch floor.

The next summer, Frances was away at camp. Kate and her mother were at the farm; this year her father was teaching summer school and only came up weekends. Bill had his driver's license. Evenings, he took Kate to the Frosty Bear for ice cream, the Moon Light Drive-In for a movie. Afterward, they walked into the woods and climbed to the deer blind, their hide-out, their secret treehouse. One night his warm fingers slipped under her shirt and fondled her breasts. She was the one who unzipped her jeans and placed his hand low on her belly. *We shouldn't, Katy,* he said, as she reached between his legs. *We shouldn't,* he said, slipping his fingers under the waistband of her white cotton panties. And they didn't, not quite. The rest of those summer nights they explored and excited each other right to the limit of the final intimacy he would not dare. Now, looking back, Kate thought there had never again been anything quite as arousing as their longing and holding back. And marveled at how kind and generous he'd been, protecting her from what they wanted.

After that summer she was never at the farm again for any length of time. Kate joined Frances at sleep away camp and, even when the girls were home, the family stayed in town except for occasional weekends. She saw Bill only once or twice, never alone, and not at all after going away to college. What had happened between them, and what had not happened, became almost imagined.

She hadn't known for many years why her mother stopped spending long stretches alone at the farm. Her father had had an affair that final summer, that same summer she and Bill were so close. Even after Frances told her, she didn't quite believe it until their demented mother plaintively, repetitively, accused their father of being with his mistress Ivy when he stepped away from her for an errand, for respite. It made her uncomfortable that she herself was now someone's Ivy, so she tried not to think about it. She'd grown so good, with practice, at not thinking about who she was, what she was doing.

Kate put on her father's old army jacket, her mother's boots, and walked across the meadow. She climbed into the deer blind and found it in good repair. Bill and his boy must still use it. She lay and looked at the tracery of bare branches against the sky.

She stopped on her way into Bedford to fill the water jug at the village drinking trough, parked behind the courthouse and walked through the square. The Union soldier stood on his pedestal, looking down on the courthouse, the two churches, the post office. The town houses of Lawyers' Row framed two sides of the square. She checked the attorney's address and walked along the row until she found his name on a polished brass plate beside the door.

Frances sat in the unattended waiting room, tapping her toe and ruffling through a magazine. *So tense, if you threw a dime at her it would bounce back,* their mother would have said.

"What took you?" Frances asked.

"A pipe's broken."

"Did you call the hardware?"

"Bill stopped. He said he'd fix it."

"Oh, Mr. Fix It. Right out of a James Taylor song, isn't he?"

Before Kate could retort, the attorney appeared.

"Sorry to keep you waiting." He was a big untidy man, rumpled shirt escaping his waistband, vest but no jacket. His desk was as large and messy as the man. He tilted back in a battered swivel chair; she had seen replicas of that chair in catalogues for three hundred dollars.

"So, your father had the old Carr place for some time, didn't he?"

Kate felt her sister's impatience like heat from a furnace.

"Since we were girls," said Kate.

"He never farmed it, did he?"

Kate remembered the clumsy birdhouses her studious father made from a pattern in his Audubon newsletter and placed around the property. *For the bluebird of happiness,* he said, as proud of his lopsided creations as Kate had been of the pottery ashtray she made in nursery school and brought home to her parents, both nonsmokers. The birdhouses and the ashtray were still at the farm, unused.

"Just a place to relax," Kate said.

"He discuss his intentions with you?"

"No," Kate said.

"Not with me," Frances said.

"I always suggest people should talk, well in advance. And in this case, I want you both to know, I did tell him to. First, there is a letter."

He reached blind into the disorder of paper and manila folders on his desk but found the file as though his heavy fingers with the clean, square-cut nails were magnets. Kate realized she was staring. It seemed like years, not months, since she had been touched. It seemed like years, not weeks, until she would go to Milan at Easter, and wait for her lover in the pension he had found on the other side of the city from the apartment he shared with his wife.

The attorney unfolded the letter and read:

Dear Frances and Kate,

Your mother's ashes are under our bed.

Mix mine with hers. Sprinkle them in

the woods by the old spring. No marker.

No fuss. I am leaving the farm to Kate;

I want her to have some security.

Frances, you have the city house,

which is worth more.

Everything else is divided between you.

Don't squabble. There was enough love
and there is enough stuff to go round.
Father

The attorney looked up.

"In my official capacity, I should remind you to obtain permission to dispose of cremains. But, personally, as far as I'm concerned, what you do is up to you," he said, folding the letter. "Now, the will."

Frances stalked out of the room.

"I hate to see bad feeling, after someone passes. Believe me, I did try." He had a worried crease across his forehead, like a doctor who'd just delivered a difficult diagnosis.

"It's not your fault."

"There are papers to file for probate. Your sister's the executor of his estate, he thought it would be more practical, since she lives in Pennsylvania."

"It doesn't seem very practical to have given me the farm."

"You can always say no."

She found her sister on the porch, knocking ash from a cigarette into the courtyard.

Kate had not seen her smoke since they were teenagers.

"Let's get out of here," Frances said.

They drove to the farm. Kate led the way, like a funeral cortege out of town. She was tempted to turn toward the turnpike and retreat to Chicago.

A grocery sack leaned by the farmhouse door. Setting it on the kitchen table, Kate unpacked a loaf of homemade bread, a jar of strawberry jam. The bread was still warm, condensation beaded its wax paper wrapping. She read the note aloud.

"Bill and I are sorry about your father. He was a good neighbor. Susan."

"Mrs. Fix It," said Frances. "You ever meet her?"

"No."

"Well, you can be best friends, now that you're going to be neighbors."

"Frances, you know I can't live here."

"All I know is I want a drink."

"Some tea? There's water from the village." As soon as she spoke, Kate felt uncomfortable, as though she were playing hostess, rubbing in her claim.

Frances rummaged under the sink. Their father hid the sherry and whiskey behind the Ajax, the Drano, the lighter fluid, in case someone broke in. She poured them each a shot of bourbon.

Her father had left a fire laid in the Franklin stove in the front room Mother had called the parlor. Kate opened the flue, lit the newspaper he'd crumpled under the tidy arrangement of kindling and logs on the grate.

The fire snapped, the only sound in the room. She should say that she would sell the farm. It was useless to her, ten hours from Chicago. Sell and split the proceeds. *Share with your sister. It doesn't hurt to be nice,* her mother would say, when there was only one piece of cake left. One girl split it, and the other could choose her portion first.

"Stay the night, Frances. We'll go back and see the attorney tomorrow, about all this."

"You'll have to wait. I can't take off work. But don't worry, I'll take care of everything. I always do."

Frances opened the trunk of her car and handed Kate the black plastic box of their father's ashes.

"When are we going to do what he said?" asked Kate.

"Not in the freezing cold tonight."

Frances drove off, car wheels gashing furrows in the grass beneath the walnut tree. The phone was ringing inside.

"This is Susan."

"Kate. Thanks for the bread."

"Bill is bringing lasagna for you and your sister when he comes to fix that pipe."

"Oh, no, don't bother. She had to go back to Pittsburgh."

"Come join us for dinner then."

Kate tried to imagine it for a moment, sitting at the table with Bill and his family. "No, thank you, though."

Kate nibbled a slice of bread, picturing Bill's wife. Serene and capable, kneading bread dough, massaging his back.

She carried the ashes up the stairs to her parents' room and slipped what remained of her father under the bed beside her mother's identical box. Fatigue and sorrow settled in Kate's bones like lead. Shivering, she put on her father's plaid wool bathrobe, lay down on her parents' bed. Faces from family photographs looked down: her parents' wedding day; toddler Frances, deep in an armchair, holding baby Kate; Frances as a bride; Frances holding her own babies. She closed her eyes.

Knocking downstairs woke her.

"From Susan," Bill said, holding out a covered plate, warm and fragrant. "Could you take it? I have to get my things."

He returned with a length of thin copper pipe slung over his shoulder, a toolbox and propane torch. She followed him into the cellar. Putting his load down, he reached up and knocked on the pipe.

"Pretty sure this goes to the commode in the little bathroom on the first floor. Go stand beside it; call down to me when you hear rapping."

Kate waited in the cramped bathroom; she heard a ringing tap near the floor.

"That's it," she called.

Back in the cellar, Bill had suspended a trouble light from a section of pipe. He looked tired in the glare. "Same exact spot we had a problem, your Dad and I, last time it froze."

"Let me know if I can help," a useless offer. She was an apartment dweller, unhandy as her father who had depended on Bill's father in his own maintenance emergencies.

"Remember when we had the baby bats in the attic, and Daddy tried to shoo them out with a badminton racket before calling your father?"

Bill smiled. His strong, dirty hands cut out the split pipe.

"Solder now. It'll be noisy. Go on up."

Kate waited in the dusk-filled room by the fire.

"All set," Bill said, coming into the parlor. "Water on tap, but no hot for a while. Some air in the faucets. It'll be brown at first."

"Thanks. What do I owe you?"

"Nice fire," he said, squatting at the stove. "Well, I'll head out."

Both hesitated by the door.

"Call if you need anything."

What a lot I need, she thought. What a lot I want. "Thanks again."

"Bye now," he said, stepping onto the porch. "Don't be letting the cold in."

He drove off down the road to his waiting family, to golden lamp-light spilling out un-curtained windows, welcoming him home.

She poured another bourbon.

Much later, her phone rang.

"How are you doing?" His voice sounded thin, insubstantial. "I'm sorry not to have been there for you."

"You wouldn't have been, anyway."

"Don't start that. Just three weeks till you come."

To wait again, hidden again in another out-of-the-way pension.

"I'm not," she said.

"The ticket's non-refundable."

She hung up and stared into the embers of her father's last fire. Time was what she wanted back. Non-refundable, non-renewable time.

Duets and Solos

The piano in the family's old stone house on Juliana Street was just a piece of furniture, a shelf to display family photographs, until one autumn Sunday when Alice and Carolyn were eight. Their family had gone to Sunday dinner, as usual, at the inn outside of town. Nestled in a deep hemlock forest, the inn was an old-fashioned oasis of white linen table-cloths and candlelight, never crowded. That particular evening there was one table of out-of-town guests. Priscilla Crichton, the owner, showed off the twin girls' tall, patrician father like a trophy.

"Let me introduce the editor of our paper," she said to the visitors.

Their mother watched from their table, resting her chin on her plump freckled hand. "Like the goose who laid the golden egg," she whispered to the girls.

Alice and Carolyn finished eating before their parents. It was too cold and dark to go outside to the old bowling alley. Instead, they played ping-pong in the basement Game Room and then went upstairs to the Lounge to work the perpetual jigsaw puzzle left on a card table for guests. Mrs. Crichton came in as they sorted puzzle pieces into edge and corner, sky and sea. She did not speak to them. *No pets. Children over seven only,* said the sign at the reception desk, though she had let the twins come since they were five. "Because of your father," their mother said. The girls thought that Mrs. Crichton, with her long nose and dark clothes, looked like the wicked witch in *The Wizard of Oz.*

Mrs. Crichton sat down at the gleaming grand piano in the corner and began to play. Carolyn and Alice laid down the puzzle pieces and curled together in the big wing chair close to the piano. Their parents found them sitting, hypnotized, "As though listening to the pied piper," said Mother. Carolyn begged for piano lessons and Mrs. Crichton offered to teach them.

Mother had their old upright tuned. Carolyn looked forward to the first lesson; Alice was apprehensive. "Don't worry, Allie," her sister reassured her. "She just looks a little like a witch." Mrs. Crichton proved a serious but patient teacher as she introduced them to scales and chords. The notes on the page began to make melodies, more quickly for Carolyn than for Alice until the day Mrs. Crichton gave them a duet book. Playing duets unlocked music for Alice. Sharing tone and tempo was natural, like the way the twins' hands shot up in unison at school in answer to the questions, even though their teacher seated them across the room from each other. When the girls turned ten, Mrs. Crichton said it was time for a new teacher. "I've taken them as far as I can."

"Whom would you suggest?" their mother asked.

"There's someone good in Johnstown. She studied at Peabody."

"Johnstown? It's an hour from here."

"Believe me, it would be worth it. Carolyn has a real gift, and Alice has promise, too. I'd be glad to take them."

One afternoon a week they were excused early from school and rode with Mrs. Crichton in her big black sedan, one of the cars left behind by her husband. He had left her behind, also, their mother said. The girls lolled on the soft leather back seat, comfortable as a sofa. They rolled their eyes at each other as Mrs. Crichton repeated her stories of hearing "Maestro Koussevitzky." The best part of the journey was at the end, riding the inclined plane, two counterbalanced cable cars, up to where the piano teacher lived. "The most exclusive neighborhood in Johnstown," Mrs. Crichton said with her thin smile.

The teacher was slender and reserved and smelled of sandalwood soap and mothballs. She corrected their finger placement with hands cool and veined as marble. Each girl had half an hour of individual instruction, her sister standing by and turning pages. They finished with duets. Mrs. Crichton sat in a dim corner of the room and listened throughout.

Afterwards, the girls had lemonade and crisp sugar cookies in the kitchen while Mrs. Crichton and the teacher talked in the music room.

They played duets every evening before dinner. Making music together was as pleasant as sharing the swing in the back yard or whispering stories to each other before falling asleep at night.

Mrs. Crichton asked to take the girls to Pittsburgh for their first recital dresses.

"It's really not necessary, Priscilla. You've been too generous already," their mother said.

"It's a pleasure for me, being part of this. Please."

"She wouldn't take no for an answer," said Mother to their father.

"What's the harm? She's a lonely woman," he said.

The girls tried on frock after frock at Kaufmann's.

Mrs. Crichton selected her favorite, "The lavender is best, with your fair hair and gray eyes."

The girls spun in front of the dressing room mirror, giddy at the sight of their reflected loveliness in matching clouds of tulle.

The recital was in an old church wedged against the town's mountainside. Carolyn played first and dropped a deep curtsy, smiling into the applause. Then it was Alice's turn. The faces in the audience blurred. She could not catch her breath until she imagined Carolyn beside her on the piano bench; she shook out her trembling fingers and stumbled through the piece. Ducking her head so she would not have to see the crowd, she bobbed to acknowledge the polite clapping. Next the sisters played a duet, crushing the puffy dresses onto the piano bench. Alice sheltered behind Carolyn's skirt to take a bow. Mrs. Crichton gave them each a bouquet of carnations.

"Priscilla takes the fairy god mother routine too far," Alice heard her mother say that evening as she filled vases with the bouquets.

"You just wish you had thought to bring flowers," said their father.

"Well, I will next time," she said.

The recital shopping trip became an annual tradition, although their mother said it was a shame to waste money on dresses outgrown so quickly. Alice wished she could outgrow her stage fright. *You just have to play as often as possible in front of people,* said their teacher. So after Sunday dinners at the Inn, the girls played on the glossy grand piano for Mrs. Crichton and their parents. If other guests wandered in, Alice's fingers stiffened and, as soon as the piece was finished, she would leave the bench to Carolyn. No matter how often the girls played in public—at school assemblies, Sunday school chapel—she could not lose the butterflies. She felt nauseous as they played "Pomp and Circumstance" together for their grammar school graduation. Alice was sorry to leave the familiar little school where the girls had always been in the same classroom.

In high school their lockers stood side by side, but their class schedules were different. For the first time they were really separated. Alice sometimes glimpsed her twin's bright head bobbing in the flood of students in the halls; Carolyn tossed her a wave before sweeping past. Alice walked home and practiced and studied alone while her sister stayed after school for drama club and pep rallies.

Carolyn's practice sessions after dinner were interrupted by phone calls. If Alice answered, the caller assumed she was Carolyn and launched into gossip before she could hand the phone to her sister. Carolyn started her homework late, so Alice went to bed alone. She missed their old routine, brushing teeth together at the deep sink in the bathroom, commiserating over pimples and split ends, lying together in the dark going over the day.

"It would make sense for us to have separate bedrooms," Carolyn said one evening at dinner.

The girls shared a big corner room, with a long window seat where they had spent hours reading, Alice's bare feet braced against Carolyn's. They slept in an antique double bed with a spool headboard, a family heirloom.

"You can keep our room. I'll move upstairs," Carolyn said.

The third floor in the house was a honeycomb of little rooms, maids' rooms from another era, just used for storage now.

"There's plenty of space if you want a new room on the third floor, too, Alice," said her mother.

Alice stopped twirling her spaghetti onto the fork, her hands felt cold and clumsy, as though she were about to perform. She looked up. Mother, father, and sister were watching. "I'll stay put," she said.

Carolyn claimed a tiny slope-ceilinged room. She papered the walls with posters and spent hours there with the radio on, the door shut. Alice spent as little time as possible in their old room. It seemed drafty without her sister's clutter and presence. She missed lying in bed in the dark and talking; she missed the sound of her sleeping sister's breathing.

The most time they spent together now was on piano lesson day. Carolyn sat in the front seat beside Mrs. Crichton; Alice sat in the back, listening to her sister chatter about school activities and friends. *And what about you, Alice?* Mrs. Crichton sometimes asked. *I study,* Alice would say. *You should see her report card,* Carolyn said. And Alice practiced for hours, finding solace and company at the keyboard.

The summer between sophomore and junior years, Alice worked for her father at the paper—answering phones for the classifieds while the usual person was on vacation; copy-editing the paid birthday, anniversary, and death notices. She accompanied him on his regular rounds to the police station, the firehouse, and the courthouse.

"You have to hunt out what news there is here," he said.

Carolyn worked as a waitress at the luncheonette down the block from the newspaper office. When Alice and her father ate there, Carolyn would pretend not to know them. "I'm Carolyn, I'll be your waitress today," she teased. Alice recognized kids from the high school sitting at the counter. Carolyn laughed and smiled as she served sodas and wiped the Formica counter.

That fall Father said, "I could use a high school desk at the paper. How would you like to be my stringer?"

Alice suspected her mother was behind the suggestion, but liked his idea and began covering high school events. She sat in the back of the darkened auditorium during play practice or on a backbench of the bleachers at games, her stenographer's notebook her excuse and her shield. Carolyn did not seem to notice Alice's presence on the fringe of her activities. Father gave her a little Olivetti and she sat up late, tapping the keys, selecting and arranging the events of the week for her column.

Senior year they turned seventeen and were allowed to drive alone to Johnstown for the piano lesson. "Thank goodness," said Carolyn, "If I had to go on spending three hours a week with Crichton I would definitely quit."

They rarely played duets anymore. It was hard to find time to practice together, and Carolyn was bored with the repertoire.

"Try Debussy's 'En Bateau,'" their teacher said. "You'll find it an interesting challenge. You'll conflict with each other unless you work out a compromise—semi-legato, or semi-staccato."

They worked on it, but only for a little while. Carolyn tired of the complications of four hands sharing one keyboard. Alice might have given piano up but did not want to lose the comfort of the music, and the pleasure of the drive to and from lessons, alone with her sister, just the two of them in the car, talking together, in the old way. Who was going with who in Carolyn's crowd? Would Carolyn get a speaking part in the play? Should Alice join the school paper? *Try it, Allie. You'll make friends with other people who like to write. The editor is cute.* Alice did not try it; she knew she did not have her sister's knack for making friends. Carolyn and the piano had been enough. Now she depended more and more on the piano, solid and secure. She found release in playing, as long as there was no audience.

The sisters stopped every week on the way home from the lesson for cheeseburgers and malts at a diner outside of Johnstown, all chrome and mirrors, the sort of place Mrs. Crichton would never have approved when she was their escort. One night the waitress brought over two slices of pie the girls had not ordered.

"From him," she said, pointing out a boy across the room. He came over to the table. "Want to check out the juke box?" he asked.

Alice wanted to say, *Go away, you're interrupting.*

"Let's take a look," said Carolyn, sliding across the red Naugahyde bench.

Alice watched her sister lead the way to the jukebox through the narrow aisle between the counter and the booths, slender hips clicking side to side like a metronome. Carolyn and the boy leaned close together at the jukebox, laughing. When they returned, Carolyn slid all the way to the window, making room for him beside her.

"Meet Bruce. Your ice cream's melting."

"I'm not hungry," said Alice, pushing her pie across the table to the boy. She went to the restroom and stayed there until someone banged on the door. Back at their booth Carolyn was scribbling her phone number on a paper napkin.

"Thanks again, Bruce," said Carolyn, flashing her encore smile and handing him the napkin.

He was a weekly fixture at the diner after that. Alice memorized the menu while the couple hung over the jukebox. She passed time in the restroom, puzzling over her reflection in the mirror. The same cheekbones, high forehead, gray eyes. What was she missing?

The family still ate Sunday dinners at the inn. Mrs. Crichton always insisted the girls play before leaving. She boasted, "I discovered you, diamonds in your own backyard, you know." One night she said, "I have an important guest coming; he's on the search committee for the symphony's summer home. I want you to do a house concert here. Carolyn, play the Rachmaninoff. And a duet with Alice, too."

The Pittsburgh symphony was considering the Bedford Springs resort near town for its summer venue. Some locals feared taxes would increase, and that city visitors would spoil the quiet town. "Xenophobia," their father scoffed in an editorial. He said it would be a boost for the economy, a second chance for the Springs, and a jump start for smaller places nearby like Mrs. Crichton's inn. She was enthusiastic, "It would be wonderful. Like Tanglewood, Ravinia. Chautauqua on the Juniata, they could call it."

The evening of the concert, Mrs. Crichton invited half the town for dinner as her guests. "The half she speaks to, the snob half," Carolyn said. The quiet gray dining room was full. Candles glowed on every table, extra help carried heavy trays back and forth. Mrs. Crichton, taut with excitement, glided around the room in a long gown. After dinner she rang her wine glass like a chime and said, "Let us adjourn to the Lounge."

The furniture had been pushed against the walls and rows of chairs set up facing the grand piano. For the first time in Alice's memory the lid of the piano was open. Mrs. Crichton and her guest sat in the front row with the girls' parents and music teacher. Carolyn strode to the piano in her strapless prom gown. The red dress suited the Rachmaninoff. Alice, in the usual black velvet recital dress, joined her for a Brahms duet.

"Thank you," the guest of honor said afterward. "I understand this is your senior year. I hope you will apply to our conservatory at Carnegie."

Later, Mrs. Crichton invited the girls, their teacher and parents back to her suite. She opened a bottle of Catawba water, and filled their glasses with the sparkling ruby liquid.

"You deserve champagne! What a night." She raised her glass, "To my favorite duo pianists." Everyone drank.

"Carnegie!" said Mrs. Crichton. "It would be perfect."

"The girls are good but there will be hundreds competing for a few spots," cautioned their teacher.

"I don't know," said their mother. "Music isn't a very secure career."

"They could double major at Carnegie. Piano and something in the school of liberal arts. The best of both worlds," said Mrs. Crichton.

"Let me give it a shot, can't you see me as a concert pianist?" said Carolyn.

"Very few conservatory students go on to performance careers," said their teacher. "Believe me, I know."

Alice knew the Carnegie invitation had really been intended for Carolyn but the bubbly drink tickled her tongue and she had to speak. "I want to try, too. Not to perform, but I would love to teach." If only she and Carolyn could audition as a duo, be accepted as a package. She imagined walking arm and arm across campus with her sister, sharing a dorm room.

"Go ahead," said their father. "But both of you must apply to the University of Pittsburgh as back up."

"Well, then," said their teacher. "We must get to work. We're making a late start to prepare."

The girls memorized and drilled the required Bach suite and Beethoven sonata for the audition. Alice chose Debussy for her twentieth century piece; Carolyn the Rachmaninoff. Each week their teacher had them stop and start, jump from piece to piece. "The jury will interrupt you, be prepared. They never listen to a whole piece." Alice labored over her application essay, taking it to her father for editing. Carolyn squeezed in practice late at night and tossed off her essay the night before it was due. Every Sunday after dinner the girls practiced at least one of the audition pieces for Mrs. Crichton, as though she were the Carnegie jury. Both girls also applied to the University of Pittsburgh.

"Pitt would be a fine place for journalism," said her father, preparing Alice to be rejected by Carnegie. "You're a good writer, don't neglect it." With all the practicing, she had fallen behind on the deadlines for her column in his paper.

Mrs. Crichton took them shopping for dresses for the audition. "You want to look distinctive, but serious," she said. She selected a coordinating sweater for each outfit; their teacher had warned them the audition room might be very cold.

The audition was in February. The girls and their parents drove through the bleak winter landscape between Bedford and Pittsburgh. Alice felt sick all the way there, and once they arrived, the nausea intensified. She sat beside Carolyn, waiting, surrounded by their competition. Carolyn was called first. She emerged from the audition room and gave Alice a quick hug, "It's not so bad. They won't eat you." Then she left to find their parents.

Alice was called and walked into the audition room, feeling as though she were about to face a firing squad. *Remember, you love music,* her teacher had said. *Don't expect perfection.* She took a deep breath and began. The jury interrupted her only a few bars into the Bach and demanded the Mozart, and then almost immediately asked her to switch to the Debussy. Her hands felt like ice, but she managed to keep them steady on the keys. It was time for the sight-reading exercise. The piece was easy, but the notes swam and jumbled before her eyes. Alice could not finish.

All the way home Carolyn chattered with relief. Alice sat numb and drained.

"What will the two of you be playing in the talent show next month?" asked Mother as they drove. The girls always played a duet at the annual fund raiser for the drama club.

"I'm playing solo," said Carolyn. "I'm not playing," said Alice, a beat behind.

Alice attended the talent show with her parents and Mrs. Crichton. She took notes for her column until Carolyn, in her strapless red gown, stopped the show with "Penny Lane" and "Revolution" and tunes from the school musical, *Carousel.*

"I didn't know she had such a flare for popular music," Mrs. Crichton sniffed at intermission as they sipped lukewarm punch and ate dry bake sale brownies. Carolyn and the boy from the diner leaned against the wall by the door.

"Alice, who is that? He doesn't go to school here, does he?" asked their mother.

"No."

"Where does she know him from?"

"Piano lessons."

Carolyn and the boy made their way through the crowded lobby.

"This is Bruce. He'll bring me home from the cast party."

Alice and her parents walked home through the quiet streets. Her parents went up to bed, leaving the porch light on for Carolyn. Alice sat before her typewriter with her notes for the column but could not start writing. All she could see was Carolyn, in her red dress, leaning close to Bruce. She climbed the stairs to her sister's room, waded through clothes littering the floor, stretched out on the bed, and lay looking up at the posters on the ceiling. She imagined the couple pressed together in the back seat of his car. The house was quiet and seemed to be holding its breath, waiting for Carolyn. Alice turned her head on the pillow, breathed in her sister's familiar scent of herbal shampoo, and fell into a dream of shopping at Kaufmann's. She and Carolyn were in adjoining dressing rooms, trying on recital gowns. "How do you like this one?" she asked, pulling back the curtain. Carolyn had disappeared. Alice ran through the store and saw her at the top of an escalator. She stepped on to follow but the mechanical steps reversed, carrying her down and away. The escalator became the funicular the sisters rode in Johnstown up to their piano teacher's house. Carolyn was in the car going up; Alice was in the car going down. The cable snapped as they passed each other. Alice woke up and found Carolyn looking down at her.

"Hey, Goldilocks, what are you doing in my bed?"

"Waiting for you."

"Well, I'm here. Safe and sound." Carolyn was flushed, her face looked windburned. Her lipstick was gone and the gray eyes, framed in smudged mascara, were blood shot. Carolyn's French braid was loose now and spilled across her shoulders.

"Did you have a good time with Bruce?"

"Too good. Way too good. Allie, get out of my bed. I need to crash."

Alice went downstairs and crawled into her own bed but could not fall back to sleep. She pictured Bruce loosening Carolyn's hair, kissing her bare shoulders.

The next evening, Alice was alone in the study when the phone rang.

"Hello," she said.

"Hey, Carolyn," said a boy's voice.

Alice let him continue.

"Last night was fantastic."

"I don't want to see you again," she whispered, and hung up. The phone rang; she picked the receiver up.

"Carolyn?" said Bruce.

Alice hung up and sat by the phone, just in case, but it did not ring.

Carolyn was in high spirits when the twins arrived at the diner after their piano lesson that week. She wore a tight new sweater; the air around her crackled. Every time the diner door opened, she looked up. The girls finished their cheeseburgers. Carolyn slumped in the booth for a few minutes before she said, "Let's go. You drive." She sat with her eyes closed all the way back. Once home, Carolyn went to the study and closed the door. Alice knew she was telephoning Bruce.

"How was the lesson?" Mother asked, from the kitchen doorway.

"Fine," said Alice, hurrying upstairs to her room.

Carolyn burst in.

"He wouldn't talk to me at first, said I made myself clear yesterday. Would you please stay out of my life!" She stomped up to her own room and slammed her door. Alice's ceiling shook with the vibrations from her sister's stereo.

After that, the girls rode in silence to and from the weekly piano lesson. They did not stop at the diner. Carolyn was dating Bruce. Alice hid in her room when he came to the house.

Spring arrived. Carolyn stayed late after school for play rehearsal. Alice hurried home to check for college mail. On the first day of April, she found two envelopes from Carnegie. One fat, one thin: Carolyn's acceptance and her rejection. She opened both, just to be sure, and hid them under her pillow. The next day two fat envelopes from the University of Pittsburgh lay beneath the mail slot.

"Congratulations, girls," said their mother at dinner. "Wonderful news."

"You should hear from Carnegie any day now," said Father.

"I don't care where I go, as long as I go alone," said Carolyn.

"Carolyn!" said Mother.

Alice left the table. Climbing the stairs to her room she recalled the vacation at Atlantic City when her father had rented the girls a tandem bicycle. Carolyn claimed the front seat. *Don't steer, you're messing me up,* she shouted back over her shoulder. Alice had been relieved to come to the end of the boardwalk and get off the bicycle. Maybe it would be better, being alone at Pitt.

She retrieved Carolyn's Carnegie envelope from under her pillow and took it downstairs to the dining table.

"April Fool," she said, holding out the letter. "Don't worry, I didn't get in."

"It's a federal crime to open someone else's mail," said Carolyn.

After dinner Alice sat on the piano bench, reading the paper. A wire service story her father had chosen for the first page caught her eye. Siamese twins, sisters, were about to have surgery to separate them. Would the space between the sisters ache sometimes, like an amputee's phantom limb?

Out of this World

Bonnie reheats her coffee in the microwave and sits for a moment. The precious morning has evaporated into chores, the perpetual leaf-raking of family life. Soon Bonnie must wake and bundle the baby for the stroller-ride through the gray, raw January weather to pick up Jill at nursery school.

The phone rings.

"Do you have the television on?" asks her mother.

"She's at school, no *Sesame Street* today, thank goodness."

"You're missing the lift-off. The shuttle."

Still holding the cordless phone, Bonnie turns on the television and joins her mother and the crowd in Florida—waiting.

Years ago, huddled with classmates on the cold tile floor of the assembly room, she'd squinted at the fuzzy black and white television set on the stage; class dismissed to cheer the lift-offs and reentries of the first astronauts: Alan Shepherd, then John Glenn, famous as rock stars.

Space travel has become commonplace, astronauts have lost their stardom—but not today for her retired school-teacher mother, watching her little television on the kitchen windowsill above a sudsy sink. No teacher would miss this launch with the ordinary, extraordinary middle school teacher on board for the ultimate field trip. Bonnie's mother would have loved bounding over the surface of the moon, picking up rock samples to bring back to class. And Bonnie herself imagines and envies the thrill of lifting out of the everyday, leaving this earth spinning below; her passport expired now, her only current travel documents a library card and driver's license.

The upturned, expectant faces of the schoolteacher's family and students gleam. The huge vessel is poised and pointed up into the cloudless blue Florida sky.

Flashing numbers scroll across the screen in the final countdown.

Bonnie murmurs the chant of those long-ago school assemblies: "Ten, Nine, Eight, Seven, Six, Five, Four, Three, Two, One, BLAST OFF!"

The commander's voice crackles, "Roger, go with throttle, up, up."

"Oh, look!" her mother whispers, amazed as a child seeing it for the first time.

The shuttle lifts up and soars like a gigantic rocket on the Fourth of July.

It soars, it soars. It disappears! Swallowed in explosive billows of clouds flaming like sunset.

"Bonnie?" whispers her mother.

"Massive malfunction," the announcer says, and falls silent.

Random squirts and feathers of white vapor weep and bleed into the vacant blue.

Her mother hangs up the phone without saying goodbye.

Bonnie stairs at the empty sky, listening to the dial tone.

She's late, the last mother to arrive at nursery school. Bonnie kneels, inhaling the heavy earthly scents of white paste and apple juice, embracing her sturdy, solemn child. Holding fast to Jill: her anchor, her ballast, her precious millstone.

A Long Time to Be Gone

"Who wants the last one?" Bonnie's husband lifted the lid of the waffle iron. Dave did the weekend cooking. Neat and meticulous—a
librarian like Bonnie, though he had originally meant to go to archi-
tecture school—he always used every drop of batter, scraping the bowl
with a rubber spatula. The remnant waffle was usually an odd shape.
Sometimes the girls fought over it but neither spoke up this morning.
Jill, turning thirteen next month, sat lost in the comics. Nine-year-old
Sophie lay on the floor in the family room watching cartoons.

Their fifty-year old ranch house was small; there was no privacy, but
plenty of togetherness. The one renovation project she and Dave had
completed in their ten years here was breaking down the wall between
the tiny kitchen and the living room, creating one open space—a kitch-
en-family room bisected by a long counter. The counter served multiple
functions: meal preparation, dining area, homework zone, and nature
display.

Now, the aquarium on the counter held a striped caterpillar, black
and white and yellow. Jill found it on a stalk of milkweed while explor-
ing the wooded park behind their house, the last undeveloped land in
the suburban neighborhood of brick ramblers built during the post-war
housing boom outside of Washington D.C.

The captive caterpillar had eaten through bushels of milkweed leaves
in the past week. Everyone helped Jill collect food for the rapacious
creature. Dave said that milkweed should be sold in the produce aisle at
the grocery. The caterpillar pooped, too, to Sophie's disgust. "Frass, not
poop," Jill corrected. Whatever it was called, Bonnie was grateful it did
not smell.

Jill had propped a twig in a little jar inside the aquarium. "The book says it'll get restless when it's time to change. It'll wander, need a place to hang." Yesterday evening the bright worm had indeed wandered up and down the smooth glass sides of the tank, trailing little filaments of sticky gossamer. Jill had hovered over the aquarium all evening. Just before the girls' bedtime, the caterpillar had finally attached itself to the screen top of the aquarium rather than the picturesque twig. It dangled, upside down, reminding Bonnie of how her girls used to hang from their knees on the monkey bars at the park, before that equipment was removed to make the playground safer—and *boring* as Jill said.

This morning the caterpillar seemed lifeless and limp. Did it look less striped, more green? The once-stiff black antennae were definitely drooping. Had it died? Suddenly, it writhed.

"Jillie, I think it might be getting ready to do something," Bonnie said, hoping this was normal, that they weren't about to witness a death instead of a metamorphosis. But perhaps metamorphosis was a death of sorts. Changing your mode of existence, as the inscription on crumbling stones in the old cemetery by her grandmother's house said.

Birth, death, metamorphosis—it was all part of the cycle of life. Junior naturalist Jill wouldn't want to miss whatever happened.

Jill knelt on a stool above the aquarium. "Get over here quick, Soph," she ordered. "It's about to change."

Sophie broke away from Saturday morning cartoons and leaned against her mother, twirling and sucking one strand of her long blond hair. "How long does this take?" she asked, glancing away from the caterpillar and back to the television.

"How should I know? Be quiet and watch. Daddy, hurry up," Jill said. "You're going to miss it."

Dave put down the brush he used to clean the crevices on the waffle iron and came to stand behind Bonnie, peering over her shoulder. "Looks like a toothpaste tube being squeezed."

The caterpillar shuddered as a fissure split along its length, revealing a pale green bulb beneath the wrinkled skin. The skin peeled back as the caterpillar—or whatever it was becoming—squirmed and gyrated, finally dangling naked and green like a tiny Christmas light, shrugging off the last crumpled husk of its former skin. It had only taken a few moments.

Bonnie exhaled, only then realizing she had been holding her breath. The green pupa was turning smooth and glossy, hardening like blown glass. Gold flecks appeared, and a thin gilt seam around the top.

"What happens next?" asked Sophie. "Is the caterpillar still in there, or what?" She was already turning away, back to her cartoons.

"It stays in there, turning into a butterfly," said Jill. "What time is it? On the microwave." The clocks in the house all told slightly different times. Jill kept a spiral notebook beside the aquarium and recorded her caterpillar observations in tidy cursive, including date and "time according to microwave."

"9:18," said Dave. "Game's at ten. Better get going."

Jill looked like her father, her blond hair short and curly. And like Dave, she could eat and metabolize food without ever gaining. Skinny and straight hipped, she showed little sign of developing yet. Last year she had been an angel in the Christmas pageant—pure and androgynous. "I'm never doing that again," she had declared in the cloakroom afterward, tugging off her wings. Nature and sports—soccer in the fall, basketball in winter, softball in the spring—were her passions. She was fortunate to be growing up now. Thirty years earlier when Bonnie was thirteen, sports crazy girls like Jill were relegated to watching and cheering. Still, it was getting complicated, as she grew older. As a baby, Jill had accomplished every milestone early: rolling, sitting, walking, talking. Now Bonnie fretted, though she knew she shouldn't, that Jill showed no interest in clothes, boys, middle school dances.

Bonnie was in charge of drinks for the team today. She went down to the basement to get the cooler. It was stored, with the crabbing nets, swimming fins, and life jackets, on the section of the long shelf Dave had neatly labeled *Summer Stuff*, filed between *Easter* (a big carton full of colored plastic grass, empty plastic eggs, the rabbit-shaped cake pan) and *Birthday* (rolls of crepe paper streamers, partial boxes of cake candles, paper crowns). On the shelf below, she had packed away the most treasured of the girls' outgrown clothes in cartons catalogued by size and season. Two librarians in one household was too much, almost competitors for who could pay the fussiest attention to detail. Maybe it would be better to relax a bit, mess up occasionally on purpose, lose something, just to prove it wasn't the end of the world.

Dave worked downtown at the Library of Congress. Her part time job at the town's historical society didn't pay much, but it was an interesting hybrid position: answering phones, cataloging, doing research-for-hire projects. Best of all, it was flexible. On snow days or sick days, the girls could come to work with her. Occasionally when he was paying bills, Dave encouraged her to look for something full-time. They could use the money, especially since the girls, at her insistence, were in private school. He agreed the Friends School was good for them, pushing Sophie a bit, tempering Jill's drive.

Bonnie didn't think she or the girls were ready for her to be working full time. She did not mind living in this "starter house" in an unfashionable neighborhood forever if the trade-off was time with the girls. Although she scanned the classifieds, the library positions advertised—with the county, in law firms—held no appeal. She had worked at the Folger Shakespeare Library, before children. Just yesterday, her former boss had called to say the Textile Museum was looking for a librarian. At first, she hadn't even told Dave. But she couldn't stop thinking about it, imagining what it would be like to be in charge of that quirky research collection in the attic of the mansion near Dupont Circle. Despite all her reservations, it was tempting. Last night, as they lay reading in bed, she had broached it with Dave, hoping he would say it would be too hard on the girls, too difficult for them both to be working full-time downtown, hoping he would make the decision for her.

"You'd be perfect," he said, enthusiastically. "Why don't you apply? See what happens."

"So you think I should do it?" she asked, irrationally angry, as though he were pressuring her.

"It's up to you," he said, taking off his glasses, folding them, putting them on the bedside table.

"But you want me to do it?"

"I'm not going to tell you what to do." Dave sighed, impatient. He didn't like to talk things over as much as she did.

"I'm not ready," she said.

"Nobody's ever ready for changes, but the girls would survive. You'd still be nursing Jill, if Sophie hadn't come along." He kissed her. She rolled away, too anxious and preoccupied to make love. The bed felt wrinkled and hot, as though she were ill. She tossed all night, dreaming she left two babies behind on a subway platform.

Bonnie lugged the cooler upstairs and put it down beside the refrigerator, opened the freezer, and retrieved the blue ice bricks. She knelt beside the cabinet and loaded the cooler with juice boxes.

"Turn off the TV, Sophie," she said. "Time to go."

Bonnie carried shin guards, mask, and gloves out to the car. Jill was goalie for the team this year. Bonnie hated the tension of watching her guard the net, even as she admired her daughter's brave ambition. Sophie she understood; Jill was more mysterious. Where had her competitive spirit come from? Dave ran, bicycled, swam, but he was only competing against his own body, against time and age. *Preventive maintenance,* he called his regime, *extending the warranty.* She had never lost the weight she meant to, after the babies, always promising herself to get up early and power walk the neighborhood, never quite doing it.

She opened the trunk and held it up; it no longer stayed open unassisted. She'd had the Volvo sedan since before she knew Dave. The girls had nicknamed it the rolling brick. She was fond of the old car, no good for highway driving, but perfect for carting kids and gear around town.

Dave came up behind her with the cooler. Mollie, adopted from the pound two years earlier, whined at his heels, begging to go along.

"Sophie, Jill, someone call this dog and get her back in the house," he shouted over his shoulder.

"I'll take her to the game," said Bonnie.

"If that Lab is there, she'll get riled up." Other families brought dogs; sometimes fights broke out on the sidelines, irritating the referee.

"I'll walk her, if I need to."

"Why always make it hard for yourself?" He shoved the cooler in and slammed the trunk shut.

He climbed into his car. They parked single file in the narrow driveway, last one in, first one out. The original builders had never envisioned two-car families.

"Wait, I want to go with you," said Jill, running up to his door.

"I have to run a couple of errands. I'll meet you at the game. Good luck." He backed down the drive.

Jill ran back to the front stoop and yelled through the screen door. "Soph, we're going to be late."

Sophie dawdled down the steps to the car. "You're not my boss."

"Stop squabbling and get in," said Bonnie.

Sophie climbed in the back seat. The dog scrambled in over her. "Ouch, Mollie, your toe nails!"

Jill slid into the front seat.

Bonnie drove. Maybe she should just send the resume. If they called her for an interview, it didn't obligate her to take the job. They might not even offer an interview. She fiddled with the radio, finding the Saturday morning folk music show. Dave had started teaching Jill a few chords on his guitar. Now Bonnie sang along with the radio. *Little birdie, little birdie, come sing to me your song. I've a short time to be here and a long time to be gone.*

Jill joined in; the dog whined.

"You're hurting her ears," Sophie said.

"You shut up. We're singing," said Jill.

"Girls!" said Bonnie, snapping off the radio.

The dog continued to whine and bounded from side to side in the back seat; she needed a refresher course at obedience school but there never seemed to be time.

Bonnie waited in the left turn lane for the arrow. The new job would have to pay much more, to make up for the cost of the commute and childcare after school. Maybe it wasn't worth applying. She glanced in the rear-view mirror. The dog stood, feet balanced on the seatback, panting and drooling.

"Sophie, pull her down." The dog bounced back up as soon as Sophie let go. The signal arrow flashed and Bonnie turned.

A black sedan hurtled toward them.

Yanking the steering wheel, Bonnie swerved to escape. She flung her right arm across Jill in the passenger seat. A moment later—a long, drawn out, slow motion eternity later—came jarring impact, the thunderous crash of metal on metal. The car spun and lurched into the air. Bonnie's head hurled forward and slammed onto the steering wheel, her arm wrenched and snapped.

Bonnie opened her eyes. Sophie was shrieking in the back seat; the dog yelping. Bonnie managed to raise her head and twisted toward Jill, slumped over her seatbelt. "Baby, are you okay?" No answer. She tried to look over her shoulder into the back seat. Needles of pain immobilized her. "Sophie, are you okay? Does anything hurt?"

"Mommy, Mommy." Sophie leaned over the seat back, hiccupping and sobbing. Good. She could move, talk.

"Sweetie, it's all right." Bonnie could barely breathe through the throbbing pain. The seat belt had become a nylon web trapping her; she couldn't unbuckle it. "Jill?" she pleaded with the quiet figure beside her. "Jill?"

A stranger shouted through the windshield which had splintered into cracks like a fried marble. "I've called 911."

Bonnie closed her eyes against the pain, listening to the dog whimpering, Sophie keening, and Jill's silence. *I let her sit in front. I shouldn't have let her sit in front.*

A clamor of sirens approached; the ambulance arrived with red and blue and white lights spinning and flashing. The police ripped open the car like a tin can, extricating them. A helicopter landed on the road. Jill, inert, strapped to a body board as though ready for some strange toboggan race, was loaded onto the helicopter by medics. Bonnie tried to follow but a stocky policeman restrained her. She looked up at the helicopter, watching it grow smaller and smaller, vanishing, carrying Jill away.

"I should be with her."

"It's regulations. We'll follow in the squad car. I'm fast, next best thing to flying," said the policeman. He looked like a high school football player, chest and arms straining against his uniform.

"Who can come for your little girl? Or do you want us to drop her with someone?" another officer asked, a woman with an incongruous helmet of bleached blond hair. She crouched, holding Sophie's hand in one of her own, and Mollie's collar in the other. The dog strained against the restraint. Sophie sucked her thumb, which she hadn't done in years.

"Call my husband," Bonnie said and recited Dave's cell number. Awkward, pulled off balance by her useless, throbbing arm, she knelt by Sophie.

"Wait for Daddy, and take care of Mollie."

"Don't go!" Sophie reached out like she was drowning, struggling in the policewoman's arms.

"Your daughter is in Radiology," the admitting clerk said. A nurse splinted Bonnie's arm as she waited. Her wrist was so swollen they cut off her watch. She lost track of time, it seemed like a very long time, or none at all, a free fall, until she saw Dave come in, scanning the emergency room for her.

She ached to hold him. But just as he approached a doctor arrived— so young, like a child dressed up for Halloween in his blue paper robe and slippers.

"Please, have a seat," he said to Dave. "We need to talk."

Dave balanced on the edge of the chair opposite hers, leaning forward like a good student trying to catch every word. The doctor was saying something: *induced coma, enhancing chances.* She tried to follow but could not concentrate. Her ears roared as though she had been swimming deep underwater.

"Do you have any questions?" asked the doctor.

"Is she going to be alright?" Bonnie asked.

"We'll do everything we can."

Dave, ashen, signed the forms on the clipboard.

"What are they doing?" she asked when the doctor had gone.

"Putting a drain in. To relieve pressure from bleeding."

"She wasn't bleeding," said Bonnie.

"Internal bleeding. In her brain."

Bonnie felt her own blood turn cold. Everything warm drained away; her heart pumped ice water through her veins.

"I let her sit in front," she said. "If only I hadn't let her sit in front. She had her belt on. But I let her sit in front."

"You had the green. You told them you had the green."

She closed her eyes and was back in the car with the dog barking and the girls fighting and her mind wandering to the possible job. Her job was to drive. Her only job should have been driving. She'd had the green arrow. Hadn't she?

Ramrod straight, every muscle taut, Dave sat in his molded plastic chair. They stared at each other across the linoleum floor, across the vast chasm of narrow space separating them. The noisy traffic of the crowded room faded away. They were trapped together in an airless bubble, waiting.

Finally, they were summoned to a little room where their daughter lay, head bandaged and swathed like some strange cocoon, tubes trailing from her slender arms. Monitors blipped and beeped. The ugly fluorescent light above the bed buzzed. Jill was a light sleeper, tossing and turning, waking herself up. How could she be still and silent in this cacophonous room?

"Talk to her," the nurse said. "She'll hear you."

Dave stepped away from Bonnie, to the other side of the bed.

"I'm here, sweetie," he said. His voice rasped and faltered, he looked at Bonnie in appeal.

Her lips felt heavy and stiff, as though she'd been shot with novocaine. "Jill. I love you."

The monitors shrieked and bleated and the nurse hurried them out of the room as doctors crowded in. Bonnie and Dave huddled in the hall like children expelled from class for misbehaving, missing the last review before the critical test. The doctor, that same first young doctor, looking old and tired now, came out.

"We're taking her for another CT scan," he said.

Jill was wheeled past, the orderly trotting fast down the hall, pushing the bed with one hand, pulling the IV pole along with the other, rolling their daughter away from them along the slick linoleum. He propelled Jill away, vanishing around a corner at the end of the long hallway.

"Be careful," Bonnie almost shouted after him.

But she was the one who had not been careful. She was the careless one. The day before Sophie was born, they had taken Jill to a carnival. Bonnie, heavy and weary, had neglected to tie Jill's balloon to her wrist. It slipped from the little girl's grasp. Dave offered a replacement but Jill threw herself down in a tantrum. *I want my balloon back! Only my balloon back!*

Bonnie felt her own brain swelling, about to explode. She could not hear what Dave and the doctor were saying, her ears were roaring again. She'd had the green, hadn't she?

After the doctor left, Dave let out a strangled sob and turned away, pounding the wall. His fist thudded against the smooth plaster.

The nurse touched his shoulder. "Don't hurt yourself."

She opened the reclining chair beside the vacant spot where Jill's wheeled bed had been. "Try to rest," she said to Bonnie, with a kind glance. "Can I get you some juice?"

Bonnie could not sit. She stood in the doorway, gazing down the hall in the direction they had taken her daughter. The first time she had ever been separated from Jill, really separated—overnight—her own father had been very ill. She had flown to Boston and Dave had stayed behind with eighteen-month-old Jill. When her father improved and Bonnie flew home, Jill ran toward her in the arrivals lounge through a thicket of adults like a tiny heat-seeking missile bent on reaching its target. She'd tackled Bonnie: fierce daughter grasping her mother's knees as though she would never let go.

Later, it seemed much later, the doctor returned. "I'm sorry," he said. "There's nothing more we can do."

"What about that surgery?" asked Dave.

"The damage is too extensive. I can promise you, it will be peaceful. There'll be no pain."

"There is nothing peaceful here," Bonnie said, and then pressed her lips together to hold back a scream.

The orderly wheeled Jill in. There were no tubes, no wires. The IV pole had been abandoned, everything unhooked, unplugged.

"We don't need this," the nurse said, pulling the cord and silencing the buzzing light above the bed. The room was dim, illuminated just by the light by the sink, and quiet, without the humming fluorescent, the beeping monitors. Beneath the bandage turban Jill's face was swollen, bruised. The sheet moved up and down. She was breathing. Bonnie had kept vigil by her crib for hours the night she read an article about SIDS. The rules kept changing about how you were to put babies to sleep. When Bonnie was pregnant the doctor said it was "best for baby" if Bonnie slept on her left side. Now, years later, she still slept on her left, protecting the children down the hall, asleep in their own rooms.

She picked up her daughter's smooth, fine boned hand and squeezed, willing her to squeeze back, willing her eyelids to flutter. Jill slept like Sleeping Beauty, the drugged sleep from the bite of poison apple under the tongue. Bonnie remembered CPR class, the one she'd taken before Jill was born, and the refresher before Sophie. *Just in case,* she had explained to Dave. Each student had a baby doll to practice on. You checked the mouth, under the tongue.

"Is there anyone you want to call?" asked the nurse. "You can use your cell."

Bonnie had seen the signs on the walls in the emergency room, the hallway. Cell phones should be turned off. Rules did not apply to them anymore. She had broken the rules today, letting Jill ride in the front, letting the accident happen. Mothers protected their children from danger. She had broken that commandment. Children were not punished for their parents' mistakes, that was a rule, too, wasn't it? Children did not die first, that was the cardinal rule, the order of the universe. *I'll do anything,* she prayed, not sure to who, but she always prayed when the children were ill, and it always worked.

"You have another child?" asked the nurse.

"She's at my brother's," said Dave.

"You probably have time, if you want her to come. How old is she?"

"Nine," said Dave. His voice cracked. He took off his glasses, slipped them in his pocket, and rubbed his eyes.

"Up to you. Some families prefer not to, for a little one."

"Bonnie, what do you want?" he asked, blinking, face soft and defenseless without his glasses.

"For it to be me. For it to be this morning again."

The nurse, a big woman with a weathered face above her bright smock, stepped forward and brushed Bonnie's hair back, tucking it behind her ear. Her touch was soft, motherly.

"Shh, shh. Talk to her, she can still hear you," the nurse said.

Nurses had been kind all through the difficult night of Jill's birth. Bonnie had been surprised and frightened, betrayed by how long it took, how hard it was. Naïve, she and Dave had packed so eagerly: their Scrabble game, the Lamaze worksheets. By the end, she just wanted the pain to end. She remembered that other hospital room, thirteen years ago. "One more push," the doctor said, and groaning, obedient, she pushed the baby out. But there was silence. "What is it? Why isn't the baby crying?" she had tried to ask but was too exhausted. A heartbeat later, the baby cried. "It's a girl," the doctor said. "The cord was around her neck but she's fine." The next day the nurse had rolled Bonnie and the baby in a wheelchair full of flowers to the lobby. The nurse checked to make sure the car seat was secure, the newborn baby buckled in, before she let them go home.

"Sit on the bed," said the nurse. "You won't hurt her."

Bonnie sat beside her daughter's inert body; Dave perched on the other side of the bed. "She feels cold," Bonnie said.

"I'll get another blanket."

Bonnie rested her hand on Jill's belly, so flat it was almost concave, feeling the sharp hipbone. She looked across at Dave; reached over their daughter to touch his hand. He was cold, too.

"Lie down with her," she said. "Keep her warm. I can't because of my arm."

Dave stretched out, burying his face in Jill's shoulder.

Bonnie had never let the babies sleep in bed with them. She had been afraid of rolling over and suffocating an infant; she read it happened. Some nights as she sat nursing, she was so tired she feared falling asleep in the rocker and dropping the sleeping baby from her arms. There were so many ways to kill a baby. But nothing ever happened. So many bad things never happened. Why hadn't she let them all sleep together all these years? Why hadn't she let them have one big warm family bed? People did, and the children grew up, the children lived.

The nurse was back, spreading a blanket over her shoulders, another over Dave and Jill. The blanket was warm like laundry fresh from the dryer. Bonnie remembered warmed blankets in the labor room, the only comfort that delivered on its promise, until the ultimate comfort of holding the baby. Then, just like everyone said, you forgot the pain.

Dave was talking, his voice muffled. "Jilly, for your birthday we're getting season tickets to the Maryland basketball games. It's a surprise, but you should know." He was crying.

Light glimmered through the slats of the venetian blind.

Bonnie lay down beside Jill, pressing herself against her daughter despite the pain in her arm. Dave reached across and rested his hand on Bonnie's shoulder. She winced. His touch hurt.

Jill gave a soft, rasping gurgle and Bonnie felt her daughter's spirit draw away from her body. She was leaving, changing her mode of existence. Bonnie could not tether her to earth a moment longer.

The morning after the memorial service the house—bursting with people for ten days—was finally empty and quiet. Bouquets had been delivered all through the week. Bonnie was sick of the heavy, sweet smell of flowers out of season, some already wilting and brown around the edges. Dry-eyed, as she had been almost all along, unable to cry, she armed herself with a big black plastic trash bag and worked around the family room, angrily throwing away the dead flowers. Last of all she confronted the huge arrangement on the kitchen counter: sweetheart roses and daisies from the soccer team. She ripped the stalks out of the green foam and tossed them in the garbage bag. Collapsing on a stool by the counter, she looked in the aquarium.

The jade green skin of the chrysalis had become transparent, revealing its contents: black and orange, the colors of the monarch butterfly within. Gold dots studded the surface of the chrysalis like tiny golden nails.

Jill's notebook lay open. Bonnie read the neat cursive.

Saturday, September 14. While we were eating breakfast the caterpillar split and went into chrysalis. 9:18. Microwave Time.

The next entry was in Sophie's jagged printing.

SUNDAY. I'M KEEPING AN EYE ON IT BUT NOTHING HAPPENING.

MONDAY. NOTHING.

TUESDAY. MAYBE IT'S DEAD.

That was the last entry, already a week ago. Bonnie felt a stab of yearning for Sophie. She kept forgetting, losing track of her younger daughter in this fog of sorrow and remorse. Where was she right now? Bonnie ran down the hall. Sophie's room was empty. Jill's door was shut. Bonnie pushed it open.

Sophie was sitting on her sister's unmade bed. The room remained as Jill had left it. An overflowing laundry basket sat by the bureau, a pile of library books capsized beneath the bed.

"Come see the chrysalis! It's changed! There's a butterfly in there."

Sophie leaned on her and they limped into the kitchen.

The butterfly had already hatched. It hung, furled, like a tiny black and orange bat, dangling on the branch. Inflated by invisible bellows, its crumpled wings began to swell.

Sophie pulled the pencil from the notebook's metal binding. "What's today?"

"Monday," said Bonnie. "The 23rd."

"What time? By the microwave."

"8:43."

Sophie gripped the pencil. Her nails were bitten to the quick, pink polish chipped.

"Want to hear what I wrote?"

"I'm listening."

She listened. Trying to give her daughter her full attention.

Your Guardian, Angela

Ted swaggers down the aisle, accompanied by a drum roll, packed into his bespoke suit like a sausage—coarse man, proving you certainly can't make a silk purse out of a sow's ear. He leaves a reeking cloud of Brut in his wake.

My agent Carson says to keep Ted happy; he owns every paper my column appears in. He doesn't own me, I remind Carson. Who smirks. Irritating, irritating man!

But aren't they all?

Another drum roll as Ted struts to the podium. Such theatrics! You'd think we'd gathered for the Emmys or the Oscars. I'd had half a mind to boycott this entire circus, to refuse to be nominated. To refuse to attend.

Carson said absence would be commercial suicide.

I don't care about Commerce, I told him, ready to take a stand, fall on my sword. I'm a writer, a professional Advice Columnist, in case you've forgotten.

He warned me if I opted out it would be bad form, look as though I was upset over not winning last year. At least he made no mention of the year before, and all the years before.

"You know I'm not a bad sport," I told him. "I'll be there."

Though I'd *never* complained about being passed over, last year was an especially Bitter Pill, I'll admit it. Humiliating, bested by that young flashy flibbertigibbet who styles herself a "Specialist in Workplace Advice."

I pride myself on my credentials as a Generalist. Good, classic pearls of wisdom go with any ensemble—in the home or the marketplace. I refuse to be pigeon-holed into etiquette *or* parenting *or* household tips. I choose to offer a listening ear and wise counsel for *all* the big and small dilemmas of life. And my columns, if I do say so, exemplify the subtlety required in the profession. Perhaps I make it look too easy, like any real artist. Tone is paramount: direct but not bossy, wise but not righteous, sensitive but not emotional, morally grounded but not censorious, tolerant but not permissive, experienced but not jaded. Well, I could go on. Anyway, delicacy required. No one likes a finger shaker, a breast-beater. I aim for Moderation and The High Road. As I always tell my readership, *An Apology doesn't mean you're wrong, just that you value Courtesy more than Ego.*

No, I NEVER complained about being passed over. *Life isn't fair,* as I tell my readers in one of my very most popular, oft-reprinted and anthologized columns. *How you handle Injustice is a true measure of Character.*

And tonight, whatever the outcome, I will neither gloat nor pout. A true Lady—and I'm one, representative of a Dying Breed—never looks like she's swallowed a canary, nor tasted sour grapes.

Oh, goodness! Now there's a whole chorus line of dancers in white gloves and hats with veils shimmying across the stage. It almost makes me feel like they're poking fun at my trademark gloves and hat, though that would be to take it too personally, of course. *It's not always about you,* as I remind my readers.

"Good evening, Ladies and Gentleman!" Ted's face, slathered in makeup, looks leathery and grotesque, projected on the screens above the proscenium.

I insisted on doing my own foundation, rouge, dusting of powder and red lipstick. I want to look like *myself* when I'm magnified and multiplied up on the big screen, accepting my award (*Think positive!!* as I tell my readers.) And I'm dressed for the occasion. Carson argued for a velvet pant suit—but what does he know! I'm not an Anglophile but, in my book, Queen Elizabeth exemplifies how one should dress and carry herself in the public eye, and I've taken cues from her for—well quite a few years. Real ladies, like Elizabeth and myself, wear gowns to formal occasions.

Who knows? The Queen might be watching! I'm sure she reads me. The event is being broadcast on network television and beamed around the world on the Internet, according to Carson.

All my readers know I disapprove of excessive, instantaneous telecommunication. But there are exceptions and tonight might be one. And I did tell Carson just the other day I was considering getting a fax machine, as he's suggested in the past. He laughed! He told me faxes are passé! Now he's nagging me to learn to use a computer, to scan and email. To Tweet and Twitter.

Well, I refuse. I simply refuse to take on short-lived fads. What's happened with faxes just proves my point.

"Tonight we gather for the 25th Annual Beeton Awards Ceremony! Tonight we crown the Champion of Advice in honor of Isabella Beeton, the very first Agony Aunt! Mother of us all, if an aunt can be a mother!" Ted grins and preens, laughing at his unseemly joke.

Really, *champion* conveys entirely the wrong message. As though this were some sort of athletic event, a boxing ring title. Typical Ted: cheap, so demeaning. And Agony Aunt! Class will tell, I'm sorry to say, and it's no secret he's from a very Dirty Blue-Collar background no matter how many gazillions he's made. And you only need to look at his wife—number five or six. Gaudy would be an understatement for what she's wearing tonight, skin-tight sequins, slit up the side. Not to mention the neckline—or lack of one. Arm candy, I've heard her called, vulgar expression but undeniably apt.

"And now, a big round of applause for all our illustrious nominees!"

Oh, goodness! That's me up on the screen. And I do look elegant, I must say. I searched and searched for these replacement frames when I lost my glasses—retro, the clerk called them. My Winged Victory Spectacles, I call them: just a sprinkle of tiny rhinestones on the earpieces, the flaring brow piece. Since the cataract surgery I don't really even need glasses—but I feel naked without them. *Treat your glasses as a fashion accessory,* I've been counseling my readership for years. I would no more go out into the world without my glasses than skip jewelry and lipstick.

I disappear from the screen, replaced by The Car Boys who mug and wave. Disgraceful! The Beeton Academy permits just anyone at all to be nominated now. Carson tells me it is the principle of Inclusivity.

Well, I say it's ridiculous and reflects a lower and lower common denominator. *Common* being the operative word.

It's an Equal Opportunity world, he says.

Now Heloise the Younger is up on the screen—really, that hair. If her mother were alive, she'd set her straight! I do miss her mother, a real lady.

Oh, look at Chatty Cathy. What in the world is she wearing? A nightgown? A slip? She's the darling of the tabloids and totally inappropriate. Wouldn't you know it? She's brought that daughter with her. Shameless! She flaunts being a single mother. Sets a bad example for all her readers. Carson tells me her numbers are astronomical. He says she tweets and blogs and I should, too, to remain competitive. I remind him a Lady never Competes. And that I certainly don't have time for such gimmicks. A Writer writes.

Those infernal drum rolls again, and the chorus line vamps across the stage. One girl simpers up to Ted holding out a huge gold envelope. How tacky.

Ted is opening The Envelope.

In spite of everything, in spite of what a circus this has become, I want to win so badly I can taste it. And it tastes like the very best martini—my favorite drink, another classic that simply cannot be improved upon—so long as it's made by the right hands.

"And the Beeton goes to…Cathy Dufresne, the wonderful Chatty Cathy from *Parade* magazine!"

My mouth goes dry and bitter. Smile, I remind myself. *Breathe. There's always time for one breath to regain your composure,* as I tell my readers. But there seems to be an iron corset constricting my lungs.

The hussy makes her wiggle-some way on stage to accept her Beeton—the bronze statuette of Isabella Beeton with her broom.

Of course she hasn't prepared any remarks, just gushes and babbles. Totally undignified. The audience applauds; the camera checks to see how the rest of us are taking defeat. I smile and clap. Pat my white gloved hands together with just the right amount of ladylike force.

She trips back down the stairs and cuddles her illegitimate moppet.

"And now for a special surprise," Ted leers. "We have an unannounced special award! A Life Time Achievement Beeton for our own Queen Mother. Our own, very favorite Agony Aunt. Our own Angela Enright! Our very own Guardian Angela!"

I'm paralyzed, frozen here in my seat. This smacks of consolation prize. And just like him, getting in that dig—calling me an Agony Aunt. Trivializing me!

Shoulders straight, tummy in, chin up, I march up the steps to the stage. Ted sweeps me into a bear hug, plants a sloppy kiss on my cheek (smearing my foundation), almost asphyxiating me with the noxious fumes of Brut at close range. He jabs the Beeton right between my shoulder blades. I struggle free as gracefully as possible; we tussle a moment over the statuette before he cedes it to me.

The heft of the figurine is satisfying, despite the sting of "Lifetime Achievement Award," and the sly innuendo about my age. It may not be perfect, but this is my chance to demonstrate for a worldwide audience how to accept praise graciously. I will rise to the occasion; welcome the teachable moment; grasp the opportunity to lead by example. *Life is all about Plan B,* as I tell my readers.

Unclasping my handbag (black alligator, PETA be damned, nothing touches alligator for evening), I retrieve my note cards. I always advise note cards. *When speaking before the public, prepared remarks are a courtesy to your audience and are as essential as the right apparel for your special occasion.* Though I've practiced this gracious victory speech every year and know it by heart, I rehearsed last night in my hotel room. I will hit every right note.

"Thank you for this honor, but the greater honor is that of belonging to this noble profession and serving my readers. Deepest thanks, loyal friends. I learn at least as much from you as I hope you learn from me—"

Ted is elbowing me away from the microphone. Interrupting me! "Thanks, dear. And now, Ladies and Gentlemen, let's give it up for Angela! One more big round of applause for your very own Guardian Angel, Angela!"

He loops his arm around my shoulders and pushes me aside, spoiling my pitch perfect remarks, ruining my speech. The lout!

I smile, the demure smile learned from the Queen: lips stretched over teeth.

He grabs the microphone. "Ladies and Gentlemen, now we have something else for Angela, a wonderful surprise! An extra special bonus! As you know, we've been running a very special contest this year—reaching out to find diamonds in the rough in our own backyard, seeking a lucky someone with potential. Seeking someone ready to learn to solve other people's problems as our dear Angela has been doing for SOOO many wonderful years!"

Another jibe at my age. And why is he talking about the silly contest now? The Advice Invitational is the silliest of his silly publicity stunts. He asked me to be one of the judges. I refused, of course, making Carson furious but I am far too busy for that sort of distraction. Carson says I don't understand, that Ted is really a media genius and the Advice Invitational is a brilliant way to get a younger readership back. Fiddlesticks, I say, no need to stoop to such gimmicks.

"Yes, I'm talking about THE ADVICE INVITATIONAL! Well, I'm happy to announce that our wonderful panel of judges—including tonight's grand winner CATHY DUFRESNE—met earlier this week for a review of the finalists. We had more than 500 aspiring Agony Nieces and Nephews! Every one of our five finalists answered the test questions brilliantly! But the best of the best was…Miss Linnet Gray! Come on up, Linnet!"

He's preempted *my* moment to make *this* extraneous announcement.

Now a dainty young woman is crossing the stage. No one can be too rich or too thin, but I believe she might be almost too thin. Very nicely dressed, I'll grant her that: a simple sheath, a choker of pearls—rare to see a young woman with the good taste to wear pearls.

She reaches the podium and curtsies to me! What a lovely gesture, the first true Manners of the evening.

Ted is babbling into the microphone. What is he carrying on about now?

"And you are all seeing history tonight! Ladies and Gentlemen, here is our Queen Mother of Advice meeting our Princess! Lucky little Linnet is going to be Angela's apprentice! She's going to be refining her natural gift with the best of the best as teacher! They give advanced degrees in everything these days—poetry, cooking—well if they gave a doctorate in Advice, we all know Angela would be the professor! So, let's give Angela and Linnet a great big hand!"

An apprentice? I have no recollection of an apprenticeship being tied to that ridiculous contest! And did Cathy Dufresne get her Beeton (the real Beeton, my Beeton!) as a reward, payoff for participating in his contest? Why, that's just plain wrong! Why didn't Carson tell me? Why didn't he make me do it? Not that I would want to be part of a rigged contest. No indeed!

Smile. Breathe. I do both, and pose for pictures with the Little Linnet. What does that make me? Ancient Angela?

The waiting limo (white, nouveau, just what I'd expect from Ted) whisks us to the reception. Gauche refreshments, over the top: disgusting, messy Chocolate Fountains, ice sculptures holding basins of caviar, sugar frosted grapes as large as limes. Lovely champagne, at least.

I may have overdone the champagne last night, the teeniest bit. The phone rings and rings, waking me up. My head throbs when I sit up in bed.

Miss Enright? There's a Linnet Gray here. She says she has an appointment.

She'll just have to wait. I require time to do my face and hair. A well-groomed lady is always worth waiting for. That will be my first lesson for this apprentice they've foisted on me.

The late night and the champagne did not do me any favors. I moisturize, dab on concealer, puff powder; brush and spray my hair; apply drops of Chanel to my pulse points. Lipstick. Earrings. Much better! Ready to set an Exemplary Example.

Linnet proves quite charming, actually. Very gracious, apologizes, says she probably had the time wrong. Says she was just so excited, so very eager to start work with me she must have come too early. The fanciful name suits her; Linnet looks rather avian, bird-like with her bright little eyes, fine bones. Pity she's wearing trousers but all the young girls seem to. At least hers are tailored and fitted. And I approve of her striped jersey and the whole ensemble, really, the French sailor look invented by Coco, popularized by dear Audrey. I once carried it off quite well myself. Oh well, the truly fashionable woman dresses her age. Authentic style develops with maturity.

My housekeeper brings tea and toast to the study (and aspirin, for me).

"I love your china," Linnet says. "Wedgewood Cornflower. It's impossible to find now, even on eBay."

Unusual for a woman of her generation to have such a good eye. She may have potential; may even be a suitable acolyte.

"Lapsang souchong, my favorite! And loaf sugar," she says. "Where do you ever find loaf sugar?"

I reveal my secret source, and the shipping arrangement from the only real teashop left in Boston. She does seem to possess a refined palette. At least I'm not wasting my pearls before swine.

"You don't mind this, do you?" she asks, holding up a tiny little gadget. "It's my video recorder. I don't want to miss a single thing you say! I've admired you for so long."

I do rather mind, actually, but it seems churlish to complain.

"Very well," I say. "Let me just excuse myself for a moment to powder my nose."

A Liberty scarf around the throat won't hurt, as long as I'm being photographed. And a touch of rouge. Camouflage.

Returning to the room, I discover her sitting at my desk! No one is ever permitted to approach it, not even my housekeeper.

"Is this your typewriter? It's not even electric! They said you still typed your columns. I didn't believe it." There's reverence in her tone and she touches my beloved Underwood respectfully. I understand; I forgive her transgression. Who can blame her? Linnet is just—well, a little starstruck.

"Yes, I believe in classic modes of composition and communication."

"I didn't know they made ribbons for these anymore. If you like, I could show you how to use a laptop," she says. "I have mine with me." She's unpacking her portable computer. Goodness, how many electronic gizmos has she brought?

"Never mind, dear, my little Underwood and I are a good team."

"Ted says you might like to learn about e-mailing and blogging," she says cheerfully. The breezy way she refers to Ted grates. I hate to think of him corrupting her in any way. Should I warn her?

"Kind of you to offer dear, but we'll have our hands full if we just stick to our program of *me* teaching *you.*" (Just a gentle ladylike reminder that she's been a tad presumptuous.)

She takes the hint and blushes. "I can't thank you enough for this opportunity."

"It's my pleasure to give you a little advice on giving advice," I say, demonstrating my usual witty grace under pressure.

She giggles appreciatively. Such a sweet young woman. Really, the whole situation is a teachable moment: an opportunity to be generous to the next generation. Even put my stamp on it, make sure things go forward in the right way. Goodness knows we'll need someone besides Heloise Junior with her wild gray hair or Chatty Cathy to take up my mantle in twenty years or so. Not that there's any hurry to find a successor. One of the wonderful things about being in the Advice field is one just gets to be wiser with age, more of an expert. A mature advice columnist is rather like a fine vintage: improved by time.

"Well, let's roll up our sleeves and get to work," I say.

"Do you mind sitting on that charming loveseat by the window?" she asks.

So, she appreciates my taste in furniture, too. What a discerning young woman.

Linnet puts her movie camera on a tripod; how tiny it is—like Linnet herself. Understandable, her eagerness. I recall meeting Heloise the first time. I took notes till my hand cramped. Lucky Linnet, able to use modern technology to preserve my wisdom.

We settle in. People say I should write a book. Carson says it would be a good retirement project. Maybe. Someday. Meanwhile, teaching this one bright student might be rewarding. She has aptitude. Advising is an inborn gift, like perfect pitch.

"Trust your instinct," I tell her. "Find your own tone, your natural voice. Your readers want familiarity, to recognize you on the page.

"Deliver your honest opinion even if what you have to say may be difficult for your reader. Remember, the reader sought you out for advice!

"Always close your column with a nugget of something practical, a helpful hint. Everyone loves a party favor, something tangible to take away.

"Keep your personal life private. Readers need to trust you know *everything*. But they don't need to know *anything* about you."

The morning flies by. She just soaks it all in like a little sponge. Typing notes onto her laptop the whole time! Very gratifying, really. A vain woman might have felt quite puffed up by the experience! The girl is Quality. A real kindred spirit.

"Please tell me about how you started," she says, "after Sweet Briar? I went to a women's college, too, by the way."

A young member of the Sisterhood, and she's done her due diligence—almost seems to be modeling herself on me. How endearing.

I've never succumbed to the craze for baring all, but she's quite special. I don't mind sharing a teeny bit of my personal history. It may be inspiring for her.

"Actually, I first found a job on a little paper, writing obituaries."

"Really," she says, eyes glowing. "How was it?"

"I worked hard and made good use of the opportunity to show the deceased to best advantage. No need to go into tawdry details like divorces and so forth. But people didn't understand the service I was providing by leaving the unfortunate bits out. Just air-brushing the final portrait, you know. So, I transferred to advice."

Strictly speaking, true. The editor fired me, but the same day the advice columnist eloped. He rescinded the firing, needing me to pinch hit. One door closes and another opens, as I tell my readers. But Linnet doesn't need that level of detail about *moi*.

"My very first day a jilted bride wrote in, seeking help dealing with a cancelled wedding. Just between us, I had some personal experience along that line."

"I'm so sorry," she says.

"A blessing in disguise it was called off, my dear. Who would want to be married to someone who takes offense to harmless suggestions about how much better looking he would be in a different hair cut for our wedding day? Anyway, I wrote my very first column, *Something Blue,* and the big paper in Chattanooga picked it up."

"How brave of you, to use your own heartbreak. I read that column every May, when it's reprinted."

"Well, thank you. Lemonade out of lemons, you know." The dear child clearly knows my *oeuvre*.

Now she's clicking furiously on her laptop. "Here," she says. "I've pulled it up. *Something Blue.* Read a little bit for me? I'm supposed to do a blog, about our session. I'd love to include you reading."

Goodness! My column in her laptop. She's quite the fan! Why not read? Ted and Carson say I need to move with the times, reach a wider audience. And I do have a lovely speaking voice, a shame to deprive my readers of that.

"Very well, my dear. Actually, here's a little hint. Always read a column aloud before filing it. You catch eensy-beensy mistakes that way."

I begin to read aloud. Even after all these years, I must admit it is a wonderful column.

"What to do with The Dress? Thrifty, resilient Bride-Not-to-Be has it dyed and altered by a good seamstress into a lovely cocktail dress! Lemonade out of lemons!"

Linnet obviously appreciates every word. As I tell the childless readers, there are so many ways to touch the next generation besides being parents. Here I am this morning, case in point, helping this nice young thing get her start. She shows promise but not (*entre nous*) my genius, my flair.

She applauds when I finish. "Thank you so much, Angela. May I call you Angela? I feel like I've known you forever! Your name is perfect, and calling the column *Your Guardian, Angela,* how brilliant."

"Well, you know, I'll tell you a little secret. My given name is Velma."

"No! You're not a Velma."

We share a giggle over that.

"Now how about a drop of Dubonnet? Not that I indulge ordinarily at this hour, but in honor of our little confab. And a bite of lunch, something light? My housekeeper makes divine melba toast and chicken salad."

"Oh, you're too kind, but Ted wants me back at the office by lunchtime."

He's given her an office? Not that I'd want one in that grotesque new building in Times Square, so gaudy and cheap.

She clicks off her little video-recorder.

Oh goodness! I had forgotten all about it. Should I ask her to erase the private bits? No, my instincts are infallible. She's trustworthy.

"Which of the Seven Sisters did you attend, dear?"

"Barnard. And then Columbia, for journalism."

Barnard?

"Don't hesitate to call, dear, if you have any questions, back at the office."

"You've already been too generous." She smiles. I hadn't noticed before how small and sharp her teeth look.

Watching her march down the hall to the elevator with her black satchel, I have a queasy feeling, almost as though I should go count the teaspoons.

Silly me.

Invisible Ink

One thing about a Valentine's birthday—no one ever forgets it. But this year, she almost wished it would be overlooked. She had told her husband, no party. Had told everyone, no gifts, declared herself forever surfeited with stuff after cleaning out her aunt's apartment for the move to assisted living.

Meg had a superstitious feeling about turning sixty, a presentiment that her lifespan, like her height, would prove even shorter than her late parents'. Certainly, less time remained than had elapsed. At fifty you could just conceivably imagine being here another fifty years. But no one, not even a wizened yurt dweller existing on yogurt and brown rice, ever claimed to be one hundred and twenty. Although she didn't want to live to be old-old—like ninety-three-year old Aunt Helen, lonely remnant of her generation in the family— it made Meg uneasy to sense the glass emptying, not filling.

On the day before her birthday, a handful of cards and a small package from Gillian's Studio, Melbourne, Australia arrived. The customs declaration announced an "art glass gift item" worth thirty dollars. eBay had changed the shopping universe for imaginative gift-givers like her brother. Last year his offering had arrived in a similarly mysterious fashion from Japan—a pressed charcoal pencil in the shape of a shell. Meg opened the cards but left the package on the mail table for the next day, glad Brendan had defied her new "no gifts" policy.

Rules were made to be broken for Brendan, who had successfully careened off the rails laid by their cautious parents, dropping out of Harvard to be an actor. Born into the role of delighting and entertaining, Brendan arrived less than a year after their middle brother Bruno died, a month shy of his second birthday. Meg's only memory of Bruno flickered like a dream across the screen of her mind's eye: her father holding him wrapped in a khaki army blanket, hurrying away from the house down a flagstone path, taking him away forever to the hospital. Her first memory of Brendan was celebratory—riding home from the hospital, in the back seat beside her mother and the baby. A blimp passed overhead, in honor of Eisenhower's inauguration, her father said. Four-year-old Meg knew the giant balloon was for their new baby.

"It's snowing," Walker said, coming in from work. "Just for you. It's cold enough to stick." Snow crystals shimmered, melting in his salt-and-pepper hair; the gray still surprised her. Meg carefully, expensively, kept her own gray hidden.

"I want a snow day for tomorrow," she said.

"Thought you didn't want anything for your birthday," he said, leaning down to kiss her.

"Nothing that lasts, nothing you have to find room for. Snow disappears."

"Oh, like luxury consumables."

Tomorrow, Walker could be counted on for champagne, flowers, perfume and chocolate. And two cards, both a Valentine and a birthday card, having learned the hard way the first year of their marriage that both were required. She'd actually cried over only receiving a birthday card. She used to be a fountain of tears. Now Meg couldn't remember the last time she'd cried. Another body fluid that dries up with age, though her gynecologist never mentioned tears.

"You should have told me snow qualifies for an exemption. It's a little late, but we'll see what we can do," he said, sifting through the remaining envelopes on the mail table. "What's this?" he asked, holding up the package.

"Brendan strikes again," she said.

"Didn't he get your memo?" he asked.

"Oh, he knows. He was there when I decided."

Frail, childless Aunt Helen had reluctantly moved from independent to assisted living in the continuing care community. Meg packed up the apartment, downsizing for the smaller suite. She'd tried to help Helen choose—rather than dictating to her as they went through the tedious, heart-breaking process. But soon Helen had been worn out and left Meg with the dismal triage of what to keep, what to donate, what to throw away.

Brendan helped with the final marathon weekend of emptying the apartment after Helen had moved over. He arrived like cavalry to the rescue. Meg was miserable and tired after dealing with the avalanche of stuff that had ambushed her in their aunt's superficially tidy apartment. Cabinets and closets exploded like landmines: discharging cameras, boxes of slides, demitasse cups, Helen's late husband's sixty-year-old Navy uniform, his doctoral hood, the blue taffeta going-away-dress from their wedding in 1946. Helen had pressed Meg to save the dress for her girls; neither of whom could or would wear it. Meg jettisoned the vacuum cleaner and dried up bottles of oil for teak Danish modern furniture; donated the heavy, vinyl phonograph recordings of musicals and Mahler; consigned the dozen Wedgwood plates with views of London. The books overwhelmed her: double layers of books on every shelf.

"Don't ever give me anything again, especially not a book," Meg had said to Brendan before even hugging him when he arrived from New York. "We're drowning in stuff here!"

Brendan popped opened a beer and matter-of-factly boxed up hundreds of books—hard cover and soft, cook books, coffee table art books, *Michelin* and *Blue Guides* from European travels in the sixties, bird books, flower books, Simenon and Tey, Robert Frost and Dylan Thomas, Arthur Miller and Shakespeare, Barbara Pym and Henry James. He borrowed the cart from the lobby of Helen's apartment building and trundled load after load to the unattended, honor system library in the basement, although a sign forbade dropping off unsolicited donations.

"Desperate times call for desperate measures," he said.

Guilty but relieved, Meg let him dump most of the books there, like foundlings on a doorstep, likely dooming Helen's library to the limbo of the recycling bin, if not trash chute hell.

"But not Uncle Lou's philosophy books," Meg said. After his death, Helen had kept his book-lined study like a shrine. "She insists they should go to a college."

"Did you call his department?"

"Whoever I spoke to in the department didn't even recognize his name. It's terrible, how quickly you're forgotten."

"He's been dead more than thirty years, Meggie. I might know someone," said Brendan.

Within a few calls, he produced the acquaintance of an acquaintance, a professor at a community college in New Jersey. Brendan filled his Honda Accord (inherited from their father) with Kant and Hume and Wittgenstein. The next day he drove off tooting the horn, waving out the window; making at least one problem disappear, with the ease and flourish he'd displayed performing card tricks as a child.

"Earth to Meg," Walker said, holding out the package. "Are you going to open it? Might be good to start early, some assembly might be required, knowing your brother."

"Tomorrow. It will be nice to have at least one surprise."

Walker flinched, as though reproached. He was so sensitive sometimes.

As usual, Meg preceded him to bed. She brushed and flossed; lotioned her hands, admiring her wedding ring. It had been hard work at times, staying married. But now, surely, they were safe. She suddenly wished to find a tiny box on the breakfast tray tomorrow with a ring inside, the engagement ring she'd said she hadn't wanted thirty-two years ago, the ring they hadn't had the money for anyway.

Ridiculous. She'd really never wanted a diamond, and now had her mother's, and would have Aunt Helen's besides. The broad rose gold wedding band she and Walter had selected from the antique store was simple and lovely. She'd spotted it in the jewelry case, known right away it was the one, the way she'd recognized, reconfirmed that Walker was the one, when she saw him again five years after college, five years after their breakup. Tall and dignified (or maybe a little frightened, seeing her again), he'd stood apart, seemingly serene in the boisterous crowd at her best friend's birthday party.

Birthdays. Everyone owed existence to a birth day, and she and Walker owed their second chance, their whole adult lives, their daughters' lives, to that birthday party of Mary's. Last year, Meg had thrown a surprise party for Walker on his sixtieth. She wanted Mary to be there, but her son was graduating from college the same day. Walker's party had worked out splendidly, though he didn't usually like surprises. She held it at the small vineyard where their younger daughter Libby was working at the time, after dropping in and out of college. Part of the charm of the party had been the setting in the shadow of Sugarloaf Mountain; part seeing Libby happy and at ease as she toasted her father, poured for the guests, described the wines with her new sommelier's vocabulary.

Lying in bed, Meg wondered. Any chance he had planned a surprise party for her even though she'd adamantly prohibited it? Silly, she told herself. You know by now you have to ask for what you want, and if you ask for a surprise then it isn't one. She read herself to sleep, stirring when Walker lifted her book.

"It's snowing harder," he whispered. "Someone's getting a snow day for her birthday."

The floor was cold. She shoved her feet into slippers and they walked down the hall to what she still thought of as Libby's room. Walker opened the door to the sleeping porch and she stepped out into flakes feathering down, like a good omen for tomorrow, a blessing for whatever came next. Meg felt grateful for the transformative quiet of the snow. And grateful for Walker, enjoying the snow with her, his bathrobe shoulders dusted in flakes, his slippers getting wet. She kissed him, lips warm in the cold.

"Thanks, sweetheart, for waking me."

"You'd never forgive me, if I didn't. I know you and snow."

Meg loved water in every form: snow and rain, lake and sea. Walker was her earth man: gardening, building walls with stones hauled from the creek bed. Opposites attract and push away, opposites complement and contradict each other. How many times had they proved and re-proved that, over the years together? Lesson learned by now, surely.

Stepping over the threshold, shaking off snow; they crawled into the warm cave of bed. They made birthday love on the flannel sheets.

The aroma of coffee and baking wafted upstairs, waking her. She stretched and padded to the window. Outside the world lay muffled by white, the street untouched by plows. Meg hugged herself like a happy child and imagined running out to make a snow angel. One year she'd looked outside on a birthday morning and discovered her daughters had stamped a heart and birthday message to her, in a fresh snowfall. She missed them both with a keen pang. When they were little, before she had returned to work, some afternoons seemed endless tedium. Now the family times together were brief, intense: real life, technicolor life that nothing else quite matched.

The phone rang. She pounced. Libby? Clare?

"Happy birthday," said her supervisor. "We're closed."

"Snow day!" she yelled downstairs.

"Room service coming up!" Breakfast in bed was a recent tradition, one of the consolation perks for an empty nest.

She returned to bed, piled his pillows on hers, and luxuriated, looking out at the snow-covered branches. Sensible for the clinic where she worked as a speech therapist to close; this was no weather for stroke victims to venture out. Still, it felt like a special holiday laid on by the heavens just for her.

Walker carried in the tray laden with a delicate white cyclamen, two envelopes, a heart-shaped box (chocolate), a square box (perfume), and Brendan's package. For breakfast, brioche and jam from last summer's blackberries, served on her mother's china. His effort touched her. The girls teased her about inhabiting the retro land of gracious living, but why not?

"Perfect," she said, "Thank you."

She bit into a truffle, offering the remaining morsel to Walker.

"All yours, birthday girl," he said, as expected. "Life is short. Eat dessert first."

Soon after their reunion at Mary's party, in the early days of that combustive, impulsive reconciliation, he'd spent the night and she made strawberry shortcake with whipped cream for breakfast. "This is too much for me," he'd said. Or later claimed he'd said. She'd distinctly heard him say, "You're too much for me." It occasioned a bitter fight; he left without eating. It felt like the end of the world. How many times since had their world come to that end, and started over?

He was the one to hold out the olive branch that evening, calling to invite her to dinner. She refused and then walked across town, turning up on his door step empty-handed: not about to be generous, not about to bring wine or flowers and be called out for excess. Walker looked wan; his eyes softened with relief and welcome and they went straight to bed, skipping dinner. Later they sat on his back stoop, eating homemade ice cream sandwiches. By now it was their familiar dance of fighting and reconciliation. She irritated him from time to time with some excess; he atoned with actions, not words.

Walker sat on the bed, reading the paper. Meg buttered brioche; sipped coffee. The phone rang on the bedside table. "Happy birthday," said Libby, "it's snowing here."

"Here, too. I have the day off."

She passed the phone to Walker. The girls had kept them together, and at times almost driven them apart. The overlap of their adolescence and caring for her parents had been hard on the family. Today, she felt as though she were resting on a hard-achieved safe summit and could look down and love all three of them—Walker, Clare, and Libby—with enough distance for breathing room.

Meg opened his cards. He'd hit it right with both the romantic Valentine and a funny birthday card. The cologne was lavender, her trademark. She sprayed her pulse spots, inhaling the sharp floral. Brendan's offering remained on the tray, brown wrapping with foreign stamps. She hated to open it. Everything would be over.

"The mystery gift," Walker said. "Drum roll!"

Inside, she found a narrow package, about six inches long, swathed in layers of tissue, with a card depicting a koala bear in a eucalyptus. Brendan must have handpicked the card, too, thanks to the wonders of the internet. As a child, he'd slept with a toy koala, rubbing its real fur pelt bald. Probably such a toy was illegal now. "Happy Valentine's Birthday!" said the unsigned, handwritten message. There was also a business card: *Gillian's Studio. Every design lovingly produced. Enjoy and treasure our beautiful art glass creations from Melbourne, Australia.*

Meg peeled away the wrapping and discovered a long silver blade. A shimmering, opalescent piece of striated blue glass was pressed into the hilt, like a flattened cat's eye marble.

"Is it a dagger I see before me, Lady Macbeth?" Walker asked.

"A letter opener," she said, flourishing it. "Watch out!"

"Now if only the girls would write back." He kidded her about trying to save the postal service with her letters to Libby and Clare, stuffed with clippings which she could have easily emailed, as links. But Meg came from a long line of letter writers and she loved the ritual of pen on paper, sealing the envelope, selecting the stamp. Snail mail forged a tangible, visible link between writer and recipient.

After breakfast, Walker left to walk to the Metro. He'd offered to stay home, keep her company on her snow day, her birthday. But she was looking forward to a little solitude and to being lazy, reading in bed. He would enjoy the productive quiet of a deserted office. Meg watched him disappear in the snow, remembering the first work-day morning after the intensity of wedding and honeymoon. She'd watched his neat dark-suited figure stride away down the block and vanish around the corner. So much happiness rested on his safe return; that first ordinary separation frightened her. Now she never doubted that departure led to return at the end of the day, sometimes even too early, their rhythm as familiar as dawn and dusk. She welcomed breaks in togetherness. How would they fare in retirement without the diurnal ebb and flow of separation and reunion?

The phone rang.

"Happy birthday, sister," said Brendan.

"I love it! You shouldn't have."

"I didn't," he said.

"Someone sent a letter opener from Australia. I was sure it was you. The card even has a koala on it."

"Guess you have another admirer. Maybe your sixties are going to be mysterious. Sixty's the new forty, you know."

"Your sister Mata Hari," she said, trying for a light tone, but feeling a tingle of excitement and suspicion.

After Brendan's call, she held the letter opener, enjoying its weight in her hand, the sheen of the fused glass medallion. The back of the hilt was smooth polished metal, a mirrored surface but too small to reflect her entire face. She moved it back and forth, capturing one feature at a time: eye, nose, mouth. Back and forth, like a hypnotist's watch. The movement, the partial reflections, created a strange effect, like a stuttering flip book of her face.

She absorbed her intuition about the giver; knew who it must be.

Meg and Walker had dated for two years in college; Seth was their mutual friend. Senior year, pressed by the future, Meg and Walker fought and made up, fought and made up. Near graduation, after a terrible fight, Meg slept with Seth, acting at last on a simmering, almost incestuous attraction. The morning after, remorseful and guilt-stricken, Meg confessed; Walker was furiously hurt. They broke up.

Meg hovered in a weightless zone of uncertainty. During the remaining weeks before final exams and commencement, she slept with Seth sometimes in his off-campus apartment. Shame flavored the sex for Meg

145

like forbidden fruit. "Might as well be hung for a sheep as a lamb," she told Mary. Her friend warned her. "It's just a rebound thing."

Meg waited for Walker to make the next move, or at least to say goodbye. He didn't.

After graduation, Meg went to London to work for a Quaker relief organization, Seth to Montana to apprentice with a glass-blower, Walker to business school.

Long-distance phone calls were expensive, a transatlantic call cost a fortune. Meg and Seth wrote letters. Sleeping with him had been impulse but falling in love by aerogramme developed gradually over the months, like a serial story they were writing together, exchanging chapters. Good in bed, they were better as passionate pen pals, pining for each other, lusting for each across the barrier of distance.

And now across the distance of time he'd remembered her birthday! The letter opener was Seth's anonymous, coded reference to their once-upon-a-time romance by mail.

Meg ran her finger along the dull blade, remembered slitting open frail blue airmail envelopes with the Swiss army knife Seth had given her for Christmas. He'd come to England for the holiday; he'd left Montana and was moving to Boston to work in a hospital lab. They spent the week in bed in her chilly flat, getting up only to feed the gas meter with coins and make runs to the shops for groceries. After he'd left, she missed him with an intense physical yearning worse than homesickness. Letters flew back and forth across the ocean.

She quit her job and flew to Boston to surprise him, calling from Logan Airport.

"I'm here!"

His double bed barely fit his room in the group house; they had never had the freedom of such a bed before. She job-hunted and surprised him again with her news: a position as an administrative assistant at the local chapter of Amnesty International.

"But aren't you going back to London?"

146

Humiliated, she absorbed the enormity of her mistake. There was no permanent place for her in his room, nor at the group house dinner table. She found a small apartment on the top floor of a triple-decker in East Cambridge. They spent weekends together, shuttling between places. She felt superfluous at his house, lonely in her apartment.

Summer came; sometimes she climbed up the three flights of stairs after work and discovered her candles drooping like wilted flower stems. Meg and Seth escaped the city heat on weekends at Walden Pond. Swimming across the pond was like making love, the deep water a place, like bed, where the growing tension between them disappeared. But the simple earth-bound things, walking and talking, became awkward. He walked too fast on his long legs, she talked too much.

One afternoon, easy and cool and wet from the pond, holding hands on the way back to his car, he said he'd decided on the MD-PhD program in St. Louis. He would move in the fall.

"I'll miss you," he said. "But we can write. Visit."

"I should have stayed in England, if what you want is a pen pal."

"Sorry, Meg. But I need someone strong enough to stand up to me."

They reached his car and she slammed her door the way he hated. "Strong enough for you?"

Meg burnt Seth's air letters in a ritual purge. She began to work on applications to graduate school. Meg went on with her life, emphatically on with her life.

Not long after she began the speech therapy program, Meg attended the birthday party where Walker appeared—like a mirage, an oasis. He looked familiar, but grown-up, patrician in his khakis and pressed shirt. "A tall-dark handsome stranger, but I know him!" she told Mary. She married him within the year—before anything else could happen, before she could make any more mistakes.

Meg sent Seth a wedding announcement—a declaration of independence. Proving to him that she was happy.

They'd only seen each other once after she married. He called. He was in town, interviewing. Would she like to meet for coffee?

She didn't tell Walker. Why upset him? There was nothing to fear—three months pregnant, she felt secure and unassailable.

Waiting, sipping a cappuccino, her hand trembled. Seth stepped in, stooping beneath the low ceiling. She'd forgotten his extravagant height. He reached across the tiny table and wiped away a dab of milk foam above her lip—the only time they touched that day, the last time they ever touched.

"You look great," he said.

"I'm pregnant," she boasted. "How are you?"

"Not pregnant," he said, with his lopsided grin. "But I have a girlfriend, met her during rotation in the psych hospital. A psych-nurse, not a patient." She'd forgotten how his eyes crinkled, when he smiled. "She loves mountain climbing."

Afterward she told Mary. "Ridiculous, but I'm jealous."

"Just visualize mountain climbing and winter camping," her friend consoled her.

Clare was born; two years later Libby came. The babies engulfed Meg. Seth sent a postcard announcing his wedding—an outdoor celebration on a mountaintop. She didn't even feel a tiny twinge, she told Mary, pleased at her acquired immunity.

Walker's job took them to Washington. Despite distance, Mary and Meg continued to support each other through irritations and urgencies with husbands and jobs, toddlers, and teens. Ten years ago, when Meg's father died, a condolence card arrived. There was no return address, no name on the envelope but Meg recognized his writing.

I saw your dad's obit in the Times. *I had no idea what an accomplished guy he was. I only met him that one weekend at your house.*

She remembered creeping down the hallway to the guestroom, unable to resist, despite her insomniac father reading downstairs.

Meg read the note to Mary. "It's funny how glad I am to hear from him. With Daddy gone, I seem to want everyone back who was ever important to me."

"Careful," her friend said.

He'd included his e-mail. Invisible, virtual ink has its uses. For a time, messages volleyed back and forth between Meg and Seth: airbrushed versions of family lives, careful references to their spouses. He had twin boys, younger than her daughters. Hearing from him was dangerous and sweet, like relapsing into an old addiction. But really it was just resuming a friendship, pen-pals again, all very proper.

But the thrill when she saw his name in her in-box was improper. And it was improper, not telling Walker. And impropriety was exactly where she and Seth had started, all the years ago, sleeping with each other, betraying Walker.

Seth wrote they would be in D.C. Visiting his sister, and his wife's family. Perhaps they could meet?

She called Mary.

"Does he mean the families, or just the two of you?"

"I don't know," Meg said.

"What do you want to do?"

"If we set up a rendezvous," Meg said, trying to laugh, "he would walk right by me. I'm like one of those FBI posters—the suspect aged by computer."

"He'll be older, too," Mary said.

Meg neither accepted nor rejected Seth's suggestion, she simply ignored it. The correspondence dwindled away into the ether. She changed e-mails and didn't carry over his address from her contacts: a covert gesture of faithfulness, to Walker, her marriage, her life.

"I feel liberated. Like an alcoholic pouring the booze out," she told Mary.

"Good girl," her friend replied.

But for a time, the world had seemed a little drab, without the hint of danger and misbehavior in it.

The luminous blue glass ornament on the letter opener's hilt glinted at her like an eye spying on her life. She held the cool glass against her cheek.

The phone rang. Meg snatched it up, as though it might be Seth by telepathy.

"Happy Birthday to you," Mary sang. "So? Is sixty really the new forty?"

"That's what my brother says. You'll find out. So far so good, I have a snow day."

"Snowing here, too, but Boston doesn't shut down for a few flakes. How are you celebrating?"

"Spending the day in bed. Walker's bringing home lobster and bubbly, if the stores stay open." They'd had a fight the last time they went out to dinner on her birthday; the fixed *Lover's Menu* had been awful, the service slow. "Restaurants are a madhouse on Valentine's. More romantic at home in front of the fire."

"Sweet. We're postponing till the weekend. Rick's in Providence anyway," said Mary.

"Seth sent me something, anonymously," Meg whispered, as though she might be overheard.

"You're kidding!"

"Remember he did glass blowing? Our letters? It's a letter opener, with a glass decoration."

Silence. Had the call had been dropped?

"Mary?"

"The Etsy woman must have forgotten to put my name on the card. Flakey artist."

Meg bumped back to earth. Her wrinkled skin settling around her like a deflated parachute.

Laugh or cry, she told herself. Which?

"Sorry to burst your bubble," said Mary

Meg managed to laugh. "No fool like an old fool."

She shut the letter opener away in her bedside table drawer. Fool enough to feel a stab of disappointment. And just old enough to wonder. Could Mary be lying, to protect her from doing something—foolish?

Never After

"**Surprise!**" her supervisor said, lifting a plastic goblet of champagne.

The attention, the sheet cake, the toasts, embarrassed Meg. No one would have known she was getting remarried if she hadn't told Jim, the department secretary, why she was taking Friday off. Walking into the lunchroom, she'd expected the weekly department meeting. Her colleagues had worked fast behind her back, transforming the room with crepe paper and bright plastic tablecloths. The effort touched her. It had been ages since the short-staffed, hard-pressed speech department had a cause for celebration other than the increasingly frequent subtractions of retirements, some voluntary and some not, as insurance reimbursement grew ever more meager and the clinic reorganized. The biggest recent event had been her colleague Joyce's memorial service last year. She'd died fast (at what Meg now thought of as young, just sixty) of a cruel orphan cancer, too rare for funding for clinical trials.

Meg and Joyce had started at the clinic together; been next-door neighbors on the corridor for almost twenty-five years. They'd been each other's on-site support system, checking in each morning, visiting together at the end of most days—after each wrote the last note, on the last client session, and coded the last voucher for patient accounts.

Joyce would have put the kibosh on the department celebration, let Meg quietly sneak off on Friday to retie the marital knot. Though she would surely have asked Meg if remarrying were wise. Kind and honest, with clients, and everyone else, Joyce did not hesitate to speak her mind. Meg missed her occasional tart reminders to put the brakes on. Just last night Meg had done something that would have made Joyce roll her eyes in not-so-mock despair.

She'd sent Seth an e-mail.

He was the path-not-taken love of her youth. A wrong path, likely a dead-end path, but still a haunting one. They hadn't seen each other in over thirty years but occasionally reached out at hinge moments of change and transition; an intermittent exchange begun when Meg sent him her own wedding announcement, and the next year, a birth announcement. He'd sent her a postcard when he was about to get married, "I wanted you to hear from me, not the Class Notes." Then long silence. The times and modes of communication changed; they had had a brief flurry of e-mail after her father died twenty years back. Radio silence since, or internet silence.

But it had always been gains and success—more than loss or failure—that she wanted to share, and maybe that was true for him, too. Maybe that accounted for the lapse in even the once or twice a decade communication. Now things seemed to be winding down, rather than winding up. Meg hadn't told him three years ago when she and Walker divorced, until last night, when on impulse she searched and found his e-mail address in a defunct account. *Thought of you. I know it's been a long time. The bad news is, Walker and I got divorced. The good news is, we're getting married again. Finally getting it right this time, I hope!* Striking a casual, ironic tone. Skipping over the pain, the uncertainty; curating the news.

And now, when she heard back from him, if she heard back from him, that would be it. The end. She'd erase the contact information. What was she trying to prove herself (or to him) by announcing she and Walker were taking another chance on happily ever after?

The day of the party was also Meg's late night at work. Everyone was required to work one night a week, till nine, so clients could come after work. Rumor had it they'd be working two evenings and even Saturdays soon.

Drinking at two in the afternoon caught up with her. After her seven o'clock client left, Meg put her head down on her desk and closed her eyes for a ten-minute cat nap before the last session of the evening.

The phone rang. "Your client's here," said Jim. He worked full time as the department secretary, moonlighting as their evening receptionist. Wages weren't great for clinicians, and worse for support staff.

"Thanks. See you tomorrow."

Jim was such a bright, capable underachiever; he could have been running the clinic. (And she wished he was, instead of the new chief executive who reminded her of a used car salesman!) Jim didn't have a car. Worried about him bicycling late, Meg had encouraged him to leave once her last appointment was checked in. She was the only one who worked Tuesday night, but was never alone in the building, or not for long, once the cleaners arrived with their two young children in pajamas.

Meg kept her door open after her last client and invited the children in to play with the blocks and crayons on her shelf while she wrote her notes.

Meg took off her glasses and rubbed the bridge of her nose. She'd have to focus tonight, really attend. Her last client was a young stroke survivor, a loner, and a lonely one. Sally had managed to go back to work but needed the twice monthly sessions, for repetition and rehearsal and, most importantly, for moral support and encouragement—hard to code and harder to justify in the notes for insurance. Sometimes Meg felt like a deflating life raft by the end of the session; this evening she felt that way before it even began. Which must be how Sally felt herself. Life was hard for her, and if it was hard to sit with her sometimes, well Meg just needed to suck it up and do it. It was her job. It was a sacred trust.

The fluorescent lights buzzed above an empty lobby. Sally wasn't waiting on her usual chair. Had she stepped behind the new partition? It screened the back of the room for clients who wanted privacy, which Meg supported, but not being able to see who was there tonight made Meg uneasy. She might have to consider asking Jim to stay a bit longer next week, just until she brought the final client back to her office.

"Hi," she said rounding the corner of the partition.

Sally wasn't there. Instead, it was a new client, a stranger.

The young man looked up at her, raw-boned, a sharp face, curly hair. His skin was ruddy with health and outdoor exercise.

Funny, that she'd just been thinking of Seth; this man looked like him. Well, the way she remembered him.

He stood up. Unfolded really, like a loose-limbed marionette, the clogging puppet she'd seen dancing at a craft festival. He dressed the way Seth had, too, in jeans and T-shirt, though the slogan was current: *Good Planets are Hard to Find.*

He didn't hold out the receipt for his co-payment, nor the required intake form for first appointments. She hoped Jim had kept both. Meg was almost certain there hadn't been an intake on her schedule, but the new centralized computer appointment system had plenty of kinks to work out. Previously, each clinician had managed her own calendar. Meg never scheduled intakes for the last hour of the evening: she was too tired, and it was a potential risk to be alone in the building with a stranger.

Oh well, at least this time her gut told her this man posed no danger. Except the danger of reminding her of Seth. She'd have to be on guard for that, in their sessions.

The surprise of the resemblance felt like an ambush. There'd been an actual ambush once, not long after Seth and Meg broke up, before she was back with Walker (what a history she and her husband had of breaking up and reconciling...were they doing the right thing?).

Meg had gone for a Sunday hike around the reservoir, a break from working on her graduate school applications. The sky had been brilliant autumn blue, the air clear and crisp. Gold leaves were drifting down, an arrowhead of geese crossed over the water.

A dog bounded straight to her, barking, friendly. She'd knelt on the path and held his strong smooth head, let him lick her face.

A woman's voice called. "Beau!"

And then another voice. A man's voice, familiar and unmistakable. "Beau!"

She released the dog and scrambled to her feet as Seth and a woman (even taller than he was) appeared. The dog loped back to them.

Meg and Seth had broken up when he'd left for St. Louis in August. What was he doing here, back on her territory? With someone else?

Fall break visit, he'd said, not introducing the woman.

Meg shook herself back to the present. The new client was looking at her intently with bright blue eyes. Bright as Seth's. How long had she been standing here in reverie? Was she having some sort of a seizure?

She led him back to her office.

"Where should I sit?" he asked, speaking clearly, with no obvious speech deficit. Even the voice reminded her of Seth: a hint of the Midwest. He studied the three chairs as though choosing where to sit were an exotic problem.

She claimed her high-backed swiveling desk chair. "Either of those is fine."

He sat, folded his height like a collapsing telescope, in the chair closest to her desk. The awkward gracefulness of his movements reminded her of the snapshot she might still have somewhere: Seth at the zoo, eyeball to eyeball with a baby giraffe: two gawky, lovely creatures.

"What brings you in?" she asked, taking up her pad and pencil. Some subtle problem with speaking, or speaking in public, perhaps? Listen, she reminded herself. Attend. But it would be hard. She felt as though she knew the man's large hands, the slightly spatulate thumb, the dust of freckles, the golden hairs, the reddened ridge of knuckles.

Inhale, she told herself. Meg blinked and breathed, composing herself.

Opened her eyes.

He was gone. Her long-time client Sallie sat squeezed into her usual chair, sniffling into a tissue.

Finally, mercifully, the long hour was over. Meg saw Sally out and returned to her desk. She must make an appointment with her primary care tomorrow. Maybe ask for a referral to a neurologist. It might just be

155

fatigue and anxiety about whether, really, she and Walker were doing the right thing, remarrying. It had been so terribly hard to separate.

She signed onto her computer. She'd log Sallie's session and go home.

New message blinked the insistent envelope icon for her personal e-mail.

Meg clicked.

I'm sorry to tell you that my husband Seth died earlier this month, in a climbing accident. Just today found your message when I got access to his e-mail. Didn't know the two of you were still in touch. Best wishes on your marriage. Remarriage, I guess it is. He's mentioned you both, from time to time. I'm sure he would have been happy to hear the news. I send you best wishes on his behalf.

Meg stared at the empty chair beside her desk.

Till death do us part.

Walker had proposed on bended knee this time, with an engagement ring. "Till death do us part," he had said.

Which might not be all that long, you never know. At least there wouldn't be much time to hurt each other again.

It was time to be grateful that once more, one last time, they'd found their way back to each other. Old enough, now, to know what they were doing.

Time to hold onto each other, to their shared life. There was time yet for joy and surprises and celebration.

Better to go together than alone, whether gentle or fierce, into the inevitable night.

Ruby

Pete sat in the furnished room, bland as a motel. Here he was, unpacked, cut loose, almost as though he'd died already.

But Ruby had been the one to do that.

Cooking had been the first sign, or the first he'd let himself see, five years back. Just in from turning over the garden, the wet smell of spring on his shoes and his hands, he found her staring at the chicken in the Styrofoam tray, blue eyes blank as Orphan Annie's.

He followed her recipe in the church ladies' cookbook for *Ruby's Fried Chicken*. He did everything, the Crisco, the paper bag with the seasoned flour. It turned out, not the same, but okay.

"Eat sweetheart," he coaxed.

Perplexed, a crease of worry on her brow as though figuring out a difficult problem, she said, "I just don't seem to have much of an appetite." Night after night, taking little bites like an obedient child, then chasing rice and peas around her plate with an intensity reminiscent of her hover above the cribbage board—competitive and intent on beating him. He wasn't her opponent though, and this game was dead serious, odds stacked against them both. But he was smug at first, about the cooking, old dog with his new trick. Who would have thought an out-to-pasture shop teacher would end up learning home arts? He never attempted *Ruby's Sweet Rolls*, daunted by the mystery of yeast, though he craved caramelized sugar and butter the way he yearned to have her back.

Stroke took her, after the rest of her wiring had burnt out. Stroke: what a soft word for a bolt of lightning out of the clear blue in an open field, though there was kindness to it. But the second stroke in the hospital carried her off alone into the dead of night while he was home asleep, eyes closed, back turned. Leaving her alone to meet it, no kindness there for either of them. He let her down. Failed to pull her back from the line of fire. She should have died in his arms like his buddy in the Bulge.

Her niece Sheila rented a car at the airport and drove out from Indy. He could have picked her up. He was fine mostly, knowing the grid of long straight roads blindfolded (which he just about was now). Sheila seemed to assume that she would do the driving for their errands—church, funeral home, cemetery—and Pete accepted. Just as well, really. He'd be nervous, driving with Sheila in the car, more likely to make a mistake.

"You think you're pulling the wool over her eyes?" Ruby said, in her sweet-tart voice, that teasing soundtrack in his ear, recovered now that she was gone, teasing him again. *"She knows you're blind as a bat."*

Sheila set up an account for him with the taxi company. (Easier to let her, but he wouldn't use it. Waste of money. His eyes weren't that bad). And Sheila fretted about the empty bungalows on either side, the house across the street where people came and went all night. His neighbor two doors down brought a casserole (helpful) and told Sheila about finding a body in her hot tub (not helpful). The neighborhood decline had been gradual. Like with Ruby, seeing her every day, he hadn't quite seen how far down she was going. When you lift a calf every day, it's not heavy.

"I don't like leaving you, Uncle Pete. Move east. There's that nice place near me." She'd been pushing it, even before Ruby got bad. "Independent, assisted living, nursing care."

"No insisted living for me," Ruby had said once, right to Sheila's crestfallen face. Sometimes she'd scrambled her words in an oddly accurate way, making Pete believe, or hope, that she understood more than she got credit for.

Sheila left, reminding him to be sure to use the taxi account, and to consider the place near her. It was easier, and kinder, to nod, though there really was no need for either, just yet. And he wouldn't want to leave Ruby alone out here.

Once Sheila was gone, it felt fine being on his own, like ripping off a band aid—quick pain and then relief.

Pete slept like he was making up for the past years of Ruby up and down and up and down. Slept hard through the night except for getting up to pee (standing half asleep waiting for his plumbing to work, grateful to stumble back to bed).

And he began to get Ruby back, now that she was gone. Her occasional pert commentary like a secret soundtrack just for him, and bright flashes across his mind like the first floaters in his eyes.

Bending her head, exposing the soft nape of her neck, *"Get this zipper for me, honey? Now don't snag it on the placket."* Kneading bread, arms dusted in flour, looking up, blowing out a breath to lift her fringe of wispy bang. *"Scratch my nose? And get this hair out of my eyes? There's sweet rolls in it for you if you do."*

He'd always done her bidding: zipped, scratched, tucked, and dropped a kiss while he was at it. Thinking back, he couldn't remember refusing any invitation (part flirtation, part practical). He'd let her take the lead, initiate. Until she could no longer act or ask, and (uninvited but essential) he came ever closer with the increasing daily intimate necessities of life. Until the very end, when he sneaked away, and he wasn't there to help her leave.

A month out from her death, he made the drive to the cemetery fine. Managed to find her. The stone was nice, big and substantial. He ran his fingers over her death date. Carved in stone, like they say. It reassured him, knowing they got it right. Mistakes happen with these things. His reservation was still open. *Peter Arthur Stewart. February 7, 1920 —.* Everything ready for him, but apparently he wasn't quite done yet.

She'd often turned in first, calling down the cellar stairs to the workshop. "Can't keep my eyes open. I've ripped out this seam twice. See you in the bye and bye." When he turned in, she'd be asleep already, neat and quiet on her side of the bed, with her book dropped, reading glasses still on. He'd crawl in beside her, catching the whiff of rosewater and glycerin with a tang of rubbing alcohol—hand lotion special mixed at the pharmacy.

Now she was at rest, that final rest before whatever (if anything) came after. Soon he'd come settle beside her in the deep dark.

Pete heard a lawn mower in the distance, smelled cut grass and raw dirt. Being mid-week, no funerals, he had the cemetery to himself. It got dark all of a sudden.

Which was how he ran the red light; red being hardest to see.

No one got hurt, but his car was totaled. Everyone drives too fast on long straight roads. Not that he said that to the police or to Sheila. But he did mention it to Ruby, telling her about what had happened, seeing her pursed lips, the worry crease between the brows. *"Whatever possessed you lamb, driving after dark, with your immaculate degeneration?"* Sometimes he could smile at the unintended humor of her word scrambles.

Sheila returned. "We're not replacing that car. What if you hurt someone?"

He didn't fight her. He'd thought of that, too.

And she insisted he move. "Please, Uncle Pete, I'm so worried."

He might have dug in his heels, but Ruby shook her head with the stern half-smile she reserved for rebuke. *"Don't be stubborn, Mr. Independent. Think of the burden you'll be to her."*

Even so, he might have put up a fight but for the eyes. It was like knowing winter was coming, days getting short. Soon it would be night all the time for him.

"We'll hire movers. I measured your suite, there's plenty of room. The corner cupboard you made for Aunt Ruby, take that."

"You take it," he said. What he wanted was Ruby, and her dressing table with the kidney-shaped top, the legs he'd turned so carefully. But it was dainty, a woman's piece, and he had Sheila keep it, too. He did take the cherry jewelry box he'd made Ruby on their first anniversary, twined initials burnt into the top. His goods and chattels fit in two big rolling suitcases.

Pete didn't ask Sheila what she did with his tools. Such a long time since he'd been able to do the stairs to get down cellar. But now, in this blank room back East, at the end of this long first day, closing his eyes he smelled damp cellar air and the hot sawdust churned up by his band saw.

Sheila had put the house on the market, and on what she called a List Serve. The realtor offered to "stage it," for an extra fee. Pete refused. It was Ruby's house. He remembered her contented fussing and nesting, when they moved in, kids playing house. Now no matter what the realtor did or promised, it would stand empty until the windows were broken and the steps rotted and one of the kids from across the street left a cigarette or whatever they smoked burning on his porch.

Sheila told him not to worry about money. Well he knew that! Hadn't he been the one to make it and invest it and save it? He knew better than anyone how it had piled up, in what the young man who did their taxes called his dooms day investments. Not such a bad strategy after all, though he wasn't one to say I told you so. He had what he needed and then some, to pay for this assisted living place. Continuing care, Sheila called it. One stop shopping, he thought. Insisted living, just as Ruby said.

The air conditioning felt cold as a grocery store dairy case. Where had Sheila put his sweater, the last one Ruby knit? *What am I supposed to be doing with these?* Holding the needles like she'd never seen any such implements before. He pawed through the drawers his niece had filled and found the sweater. As he put it on, he heard the industrious click of her needles, and her mutter counting stitches under her breath, her victorious exhale as she turned a heel. Wearing the sweater was close as he could come to holding Ruby. He found it harder to summon her up, in this place she'd never been.

Sheila had offered to drive him out to the cemetery one last time; he declined. He wished he'd gone. He wished he'd stayed at the hospital that night. You couldn't have known, Uncle Pete, Sheila said. But he had. He'd been afraid to say good bye.

Sheila brought take out Chinese to the house the last night. She read him the fortune in his cookie. "*You regret more what you don't do than what you do.* That's not a fortune, Uncle Pete!" Maybe not, but it summed things up.

A chime rang in the hall. An aide came, smelling of some heavy oil. "Dinnertime, Mr. Pete." She hung his key around his neck on the lanyard with the emergency call gizmo to use in case he fell. "Lock up. There's people on the floor who are confused. Things go missing."

He had nothing left of value to go missing.

Her hand was warm and strong as she guided him to a railing in the corridor. "Just follow this. Takes you straight to the dining room."

Don't go, he almost said, like a kid on the steps of a new school. How many of those had he taken care of? How many newbies (raw as just born mice) had he shown the way to the cafeteria?

Pete almost collided with a metal walker suddenly in his path. His eyes were bad enough paying attention, let alone wool-gathering.

"Excuse me," he said.

"My fault, I never drove before having this thing," she said. A voice like doves under the eaves, rain on the porch roof. "You're my new neighbor. Helen Czerny. Onward to dinner, shall we?"

He would learn there were good tables and bad, like at school. Here there were tables where no one talked and tables where no one could talk. Her table was best, and since he was with her (and a man), they made room. "This is Peter Stewart," she said in that soft, firm voice. Helen was in charge. He was the new boy and he was with the prettiest girl in school.

Faces were the hardest to see, blurry as though he were pressed too close to a fine mesh screen. But he could see Helen in that way he'd developed, what kids at school would call his secret superpower. As his eyes got worse, the second sight (or whatever it was) sharpened. So he saw her, this Helen Czerny, her oval face and wide-spaced brown eyes and hair (softer brown) in a page boy to her shoulders. And a soft sweater, a cardigan buttoned up the back the way the girls wore them when he was in high school. A strand of pearls around her neck.

"He's still wearing his hat," one of the ladies at the table said in an angry voice. He didn't beg pardon or explain that the baseball cap cut the glare.

Helen read the menu out loud without his asking. "Tomato juice or pear and cottage cheese? Broiled cod or meatloaf?" She filled out the chit for him, too, no questions asked, as though they'd been a longtime couple.

Later he heard Helen's television faintly from next door. What would she be watching? A nature show? Her clock chimed through the wall.

He sat in the recliner chair, listening. Saw her in a chenille robe. Smelled rosewater and glycerin lotion.

The aide brought his drops and pills. Helped him to and from the bathroom. Would have helped him into bed but he wasn't ready.

He fell asleep sitting up in his chair, like an astronaut in his space capsule spinning around the earth, way up above.

Helen was at his door when he stepped into the hall, heading to breakfast.

"Just reading about you."

She explained about the little bulletin board by each door. Read the write up about him, described his last school picture, the one from the year he retired.

"My niece must have done it," he said. "It's like hearing my own obituary."

She laughed, a sound like doves in the eaves. "Nieces! Mine's the boon and the bane of my existence. You're from Terre Haute? We lived in Bloomington, when my husband was first teaching."

After breakfast he walked her home. Well, to her door. Asked her to read him her bulletin board biography. She'd called her husband a teacher; turned out he was a professor. He liked that she didn't put on airs. Helen had taught junior high history. If she'd taught in Terre Haute, they might have had coffee together, in the teachers' lounge.

He asked about her picture.

"It's ancient. But the one my niece will use in my death notice, so why not?" That laugh again, doves in eaves. "Yearbook picture, senior year in college. I'm wearing a sweater and my add-a-pearl necklace. My hair was a long bob to my shoulders. Brown, like my eyes. I was considered beautiful," she said, matter of fact as though speaking of someone else.

You still are. Knowing it as if he could see her face clearly.

"Mrs. Helen, I'm here for your shower," said the aide, startling him. In the shadowy darkness he carried around like weather, he'd forgotten they weren't alone.

Sheila came to lunch on Sunday. Dinner, they called it on the announcements. Helen wasn't there. He was glad not to make any introduction. To keep her his secret piece of pocket gold. Would Ruby mind? Would Sheila?

They went outside afterward. The air was fresh, but the glare hurt. He'd forgotten his dark glasses. Pete felt uneasy in the unknown landscape. Becoming an inmate, he thought. He'd been the outside person, Ruby the inside: industrial arts and home arts.

"There are geese on the pond," said Sheila. "A little island with a tree."

Back inside she bustled around making labels he'd not be able to read.

"Anyone you'd like to call, while I'm here? I've ordered a phone with a big dial. And an easy remote, for the TV. There's someone who can come and give us advice about things that will make it easier, with your eyes."

She meant well, but her anxious voice and hover, her eagerness to solve his problems (and solve her problem: Pete) wore him out. What he wanted was to sit in the lounge chair and close his eyes. No one he wanted to talk to back home but Ruby. No one, except for Ruby, he missed. The first September after retiring he expected to miss school. But it turned out like a snake shedding its skin. His world narrowed down to his shop down the cellar, the garden, and Ruby. Simple and sufficient.

Sheila fiddled with the radio, finding a classical station. That seemed to make it easier for her to go, leaving him with some noise in the room.

He closed his eyes and was an astronaut again, floating in the dark looking down on the world left behind. Just needed to get a little farther up and farther out.

A knock roused him. Helen's soft voice. "Pete?"

He was careful, going from sitting to standing, slow going to the door. Called out so she wouldn't give up and leave.

"I'm going down to vespers," she said.

He must have looked blank because she laughed.

"Evensong," she said. "It's nice, depending on who does it. They rotate. I'm Methodist, that's why I'm here. But I like the Catholic priest best. This is his Sunday."

"Do we have to go outside?" He wanted to take it back as soon as he spoke, not wanting to look timid.

"Tunnels," she said, laughing again. "We don't ever have to leave this place, isn't that an awful thought?"

He leaned on the hall railing as they walked, she rattled alongside with her walker.

"We're going to Evensong," she told the attendant at the nurse's station.

From the elevator they walked until the carpet ended on a tile floor. There was a scent of hospital.

"Where are we?"

"Crossing the border between assisted living and nursing home. Don't worry, I'll get us back."

The chapel was small, dim, and too warm. He took off his hat. Her voice singing the hymns was dry and reedy, like the sound of holding a blade of grass between two fingers and blowing across. He closed his eyes and smelled summer sun and breeze and cut hay.

He hadn't gone to church with Ruby, hadn't said the Lord's Prayer since they stopped doing it at school. This priest used "debts" instead of "trespasses," which tripped Pete up.

"I prefer trespasses, too," said Helen as they walked to the elevator. "Quite a different meaning than debts. You can pay off debts. You need forgiveness for trespasses."

The nurse with the medicine cart greeted them upstairs. "I was looking for you two," as though they were a couple of kids sneaking out. She dosed them and rolled on.

"I like to have a sherry on Sundays," Helen said. "Join me?"

Sheila had read him the rules, on the papers he'd signed.

Helen laughed. "Don't look so disapproving! It's allowed, if you're quiet about it. My niece Meg smuggles it in. I have cranberry juice if you'd rather."

She left her walker by the door; surer here, on her turf.

The apartment smelled of spice and flowers, like Ruby's pomander balls, oranges stuck with cloves.

"Smells nice in here."

"Potpourri. From our roses. My last batch, the fragrance is almost worn out."

He had a blurred impression of shelves filled with books, the glint of gold frames on painted pictures, pools of lamplight.

Sitting at her table, Pete stroked the wood: smooth and fine grained, well taken care of. Her skin would be, too. "Cherry," he said. "I made Ruby, my wife, a cherry jewelry box." Reminding himself he was married, yet feeling he'd confided something he should have kept private, mentioning that jewelry box.

The glasses were small, thin stemmed crystal. Helen clinked hers against his. The drink tasted sweet and smoky. Pete wasn't teetotal, but he'd never had much of a taste for beer or liquor. This was nice.

"Tell me about Ruby," she said. Her voice, the dim room, felt warm and intimate, as if they were lying together in bed, talking in the dark, the way he and Ruby sometimes did if she'd roused when he came to bed, after they made love.

"We met at the school where I taught shop. She taught home arts till we got married. Almost sixty years ago. Her favorite color was red, like her name. She never wore black, said it made her look dead." Why did he say all that?

Helen laughed. "Oh, I like her. Black's the most boring color, non-color, under the sun. Do you have children?"

"No."

"Nor did we. How long has she been gone?"

"Four months. Dementia, then a stroke. I'd gone home just before she died." Why on earth did he tell her that?

"Likely made it easier for her to let go. My husband died alone. I think he wanted it that way. He belonged to the Hemlock Society."

"What's that?"

"Socrates. Suicide, basically. He had his stash, he had his plan. But he was too weak to do anything except just stop eating and drinking."

Pete didn't know what to say.

"So, I wasn't there when Lou died. Though it's not just about the last moment, is it? There's all the life you had before. Joy. Sorrow."

Her voice made his heart ache the way certain music did sometimes. Made Pete picture Ruby, lying in bed under the faded quilt, still and composed after each miscarriage. Waiting until she thought he was asleep to cry. And while she wept, he lay there, pretending to sleep, afraid to touch her. All the things she'd asked him to do, the little touchings, and she'd never said, "Hold me please. I'm sad." Why had he waited to be asked?

"Another drop?"

Helen filled his glass. He drank it down, quickly—it was a very small glass. "Tell me about your husband."

"Lou and I met in college, in the drama club. Married when he got out of the service."

"When did he pass?"

"Oh, a long time ago. Thirty-seven years. He was only fifty." She paused, took a sip. "He had AIDS."

Why did he need aides, he wondered for a moment, then understood. He'd never known anyone that happened to. Ruby had had a phobia about dirty needles, injections, blood work, after all that started. Mercifully, she forgot that, too.

"He was bisexual," she said, voice weary, the light gone out of it. "Have I shocked you?"

"No," he said, surprised to find it true. "I had gay students, but I was slow, figuring that out. It was hard for them."

"Well, love is. Love is love, Pete. Complicated. You know what Shakespeare said."

"I don't." Somehow not ashamed to admit it, to her.

"Love is not love which alters when it alteration finds." She filled his thimble-size glass again without asking. "It does infuriate me, people thinking because we're old, we're innocents."

"If you laid everyone's experience in this place end to end, it'd cover a few miles," he said.

"Exactly," she agreed. "My new friend. My last friend, I think."

Falling asleep he listened to her clock chime next door. He had never had a woman friend, except Ruby. It had been a while since he really had a friend, if you didn't count Ruby.

At breakfast the activities director came by the table. She was brisk and enthusiastic, reminding him of a woman gym teacher at his school.

"We're going to the National Gallery downtown on Wednesday."

"I'd love to go," said Helen. "If it weren't for the walker." Such longing in her voice.

"No problem," said the activities person. "Loaner wheelchairs there. I'll push you."

"Why don't you come too, Pete?" Helen asked.

"It would be wasted on me, these eyes."

"Push me and I'll tell you what we're looking at."

They sat together on the bus.

"Last time I went on a field trip, I was chaperone," he said.

She laughed. He felt like he'd grabbed the gold ring on the merry-go-round, amusing her.

Helen described what they passed. The Washington Monument, the new World War II monument (which she didn't think much of and was glad her husband never saw), the White House. White marble glittered against blue, blue, blue.

Pushing the chair was easy on the marble floors. She told him when to stop, when to turn.

"Good thing you're leading. I never could dance," he said. Again, her laughter like a prize. Wanting more, Pete started to say something about chaperoning the middle school dances. But saw Ruby at the punch table, catching his eye. All dressed up in her red chiffon, her pumps. They never danced on duty in the gym but afterward, home, turned on the kitchen radio and swayed around the room in the dark.

The special exhibit was a painter from Pennsylvania, Andrew Wyeth. He'd heard of him.

Helen read the brochure aloud. "The show's called 'Looking Out, Looking In.' He was interested in windows. Because they framed the world he painted."

They took it slow, stopping in front of each picture. The rest of their group left them behind. Her descriptions were so clear Pete could see the slant of a roof, the streaked gray of the sky, paint blistered on clapboard.

The activities director came. "We're going down to the cafeteria now."

"I'm not hungry," said Helen. "Park me in front of this picture. I'll be more than content."

"I'll stay, too," he said. And be more than content.

"So, it's called Wind from the Sea," she said.

He saw a block of light against a block of dark.

"There's a curtain, a thin curtain blowing in."

"What color?"

"No color. Translucent, filmy. Nylon. That's what's amazing. How he does it. Makes air visible. People says it's like a photograph. But it's better."

As a kid, he'd listened to ball games on the radio. After he and Ruby had television, he watched. But he'd always preferred the radio, listening to the announcer's description, filling in the picture for himself.

"There's a field outside the window, tracks in it, a curve of two tire tracks."

Pete closed his eyes, easier to see without the distraction of glare and shadow.

They sat there, quiet. Helen looking at the painting he supposed; Pete looking at the idea of the painting which became stepping into it, one of those tricks his mind played—pretty good consolation, for what he couldn't see.

"More than content," he said.

"Good," she said.

Footsteps echoed on the marble floor; people paused and murmured and passed on.

They weren't alone, but it felt like just the two of them.

"We're inside looking out," he said, daring to rest his hand on the cracked vinyl armrest of her wheel chair, like the first time he went to the movies with Ruby, his arm snaked across the velveteen top of her seat, working up his nerve.

Pete fell asleep in the recliner after they got back. The aide woke him. He hadn't heard her knock, or the sound of her key. She loomed over him, a cloud of white uniform, dusky face, some tropical fragrance. Helen had told him the accent was from a French-speaking country in Africa.

"Dinnertime, Mr. Pete. I have your drops."

He blinked on the drops and saw wind blowing a sheer curtain.

Pete knocked on Helen's door before going to the dining room. She didn't answer. She must have come for him and he'd slept through her call. They'd skipped lunch, she'd be hungry. It was good to be hungry for a change. Pete had fallen out of the habit of three meals a day when Ruby lost her thermostat for hot and cold, didn't seem to register empty and full. But here you no sooner pushed away from the table than it was time to eat again.

He sat down with a lurch at the table, without Helen to guide him.

"Where's your girlfriend?" said the woman next to him. She always sounded angry. Maybe she was.

The young waitress read him the choices too fast. Helen had been on the committee to choose a waitress for a scholarship to the community college. She knew them all by name.

After dinner he knocked again at her door. An aide passed by. "She fell this afternoon. Took her over to Shady Grove."

Shady Grave, Helen called the hospital, laughing. "Hope I never go there again. This apartment is my final resting place."

Pete sat in his recliner, listening to her clock through the wall.

Carmen, his favorite, came to help him in the morning. She never rushed, sat outside the bathroom door while he perched on the plastic shower bench in the stream of water she'd adjusted to just the right temperature, let him soap himself with the wash cloth she'd left ready. Never yanked the shower curtain open before he asked. Stood waiting with his robe.

He wished he'd been half as good with Ruby.

Sometimes after her shift, Carmen sat in Helen's apartment, just visiting. Helen had told him the woman's son was in prison; she was studying for a nurse's aide certificate but couldn't pass the test though she was the best of them all.

"Everyone tells you their life story," he'd said. Like me, he thought.

"Oh, we invisibles have to stick together."

"What?"

"We're invisible because we're old. They're brown."

"It's the way you pay attention."

"That's a very nice thing to say," she'd said, not laughing. He had that feeling again, of catching the gold ring prize.

Carmen told him Helen had broken her hip.

When he'd been in the service, they joked—and it wasn't joking—about the golden bullet, the hoped-for injury bad enough to send you home but all in one piece. His own grandmother had talked about pneumonia as the old folks' friend, a different kind of golden bullet, taking you out, sending you home.

Now a broken hip just meant staying on for pain and difficulty and work.

She'd never said, if she belonged to the Evergreen group, too. Did Helen have something laid by, to ease her out? Smuggled in like her sherry?

He asked Carmen to place the call to the hospital. Patient information connected him to her room. The phone rang and rang.

Carmen told him when she was brought back to the rehabilitation unit downstairs. She showed him the way there.

Her room was right across from the nurse's station. Pete got tangled in the curtain between the beds. She lay on the quiet side; her roommate had her television on.

The glare of the fluorescent made it harder to see.

"Could you turn that light off?" he asked Carmen.

He made out a small body in bed.

"How are you, Mrs. Helen?" asked Carmen.

No answer.

"I've brought Mr. Pete."

No answer.

Carmen pulled a chair up next to the bed for him. "I'll come back for you." Her shadowy form swooped down over the bed. He sensed rather than saw her kiss Helen's forehead. "I miss you," the aide whispered.

The roommate's television droned on. A therapist came for her. "Could you turn that off? While you're gone?" he called out.

Blessed quiet.

Ruby had been in the new hospital in town, all the rooms private. He hadn't even known how lucky that was.

Pete heard Helen breathing, ragged puffs.

"It's too long," she whispered, more exhalation than voice.

Lunch came. "Maybe she'll eat for you," the aide said, positioning the rolling table over the bed.

"Do you want to try?" he asked, after the aide had gone. "I may make a mess."

"No," she said. Refusing, her voice was steady, stronger.

He sat there all day. Stopped hearing the television, the background buzz of noise in the hall. He found it was possible to just sit and be there, not dozing: drifting, wandering between here and there, now and then, Helen's bedside and Ruby's.

Carmen tapped his shoulder.

"Time to go up, Mr. Pete."

"I'll stay awhile. I can find my way."

Later, someone came in. "Who are you?" Pete heard surprise, protection in the woman's voice.

"Pete Stewart," he said. "Her neighbor from upstairs."

"She's mentioned you. I'm her niece, Meg. Thanks for being here."

Pete knew he should leave. But Helen herself might leave while he was gone. Well, fair enough if she did. The niece was here. She should be with family at the end, no matter what she said about the last moment not being so all-important.

He groped his way down the hall, rode the elevator upstairs. Carmen must have left the tray with the sandwich and carton of milk.

Helen was still there, the next day, and the next, and the next. Using what strength she had to refuse to eat, to refuse to drink, to pluck out the IV delivering fluid.

"Her heart's strong," her niece said. Meg came every day before and after work. The two of them met bedside morning and evening like a change of shift; walked down the hallway toward Pete's elevator together. "She's given up. But if she'd just drink, eat, get strong enough for physical therapy."

"She says it's been too long," Pete said.

"Said the same thing to me, too."

"Maybe she's right," he said.

He found her bed empty the next day. She's done it, he thought. Without me. Why had no one called? He would have come. He could have come. Said good bye. This time he could have said good bye.

"The family had her moved upstairs," the nurse said. "Ninth floor. Hospice."

Pete took up his daily vigil there. Drank the small cans of apple juice, ate the cottage cheese the nurses brought him. Slept in the reclining chair by her bed till Meg came, evenings after work and spent the night. He relieved her in the mornings.

Helen no longer spoke. But one morning, just after her niece left, Helen whispered, "They've locked the gates. If I turn sideways, I can slip through the fence."

He had a hunch then and he could have called Meg. Knew he should. But he didn't. Decided not to, though not entirely sure why. Maybe because he didn't want to share? Maybe because this time he wanted to do it right. Or maybe because Helen had told him there were some things easier to do, without a loved one present.

Anyway, selfish or not, he chose, and he was there that afternoon when she did slip through. Not talking, not touching her, just sitting. Making sure she was not alone but not encumbered by anyone too close. He took off his cap and said the prayer very softly, using trespasses not debts before he called Meg on the number she'd given him, before he rang the buzzer for the nurse.

Meg knocked on his door that evening. "Pete, come have a sherry. Aunt Helen wouldn't like me drinking alone."

The room smelled of roses and spices but felt different with her gone. Rooms, bodies, are just containers after all. When they're empty, they're empty.

They drank from the little glasses.

"I should have been there," Meg said. "They don't give you leave, for aunts. Why didn't I just take it?"

He felt a pang. He'd trespassed. Taken the place that should have been hers. "Maybe having you away may made it easier for her to let go."

"I never said goodbye."

"It's your whole life together, not just the last moment," he said, hoping she'd take more comfort in Helen's words than he had.

Meg made a sound, halfway between crying and laughing. "That sounds like something she would say."

"It's what she told me," he admitted. "I wasn't with my wife, when she passed."

"Oh, so you know. Thank you for telling me. And being with her. She wasn't alone."

He almost apologized. Was about to explain. But the clock chimed, musical and soft as Helen's voice interrupting him, hushing him. What's done is done. No do-overs.

"She wanted you to have the clock," Meg said. "To keep you company."

"I couldn't. You should have it."

"It's what she wanted, and I do, too. Please. It does have to be wound once a week. I did it on Sundays. I could come out."

"Please show me how."

Meg wouldn't want to come, or not for long. And besides, Pete's fingers anticipated the pleasure of tightening the spring, keeping it going, keeping the voice alive, hearing the chime.

Good to be useful, right up to the end.

Fugitive Day

The sweet sharp sense of a fugitive day
Fetched back from its thickening shroud of gray.
—*Thomas Hardy*

Yonder Hills our house was called then, and still is now, after a line from a hymn my grandmother used to sing: *yonder hills are very fair*. And the Smokies still are very fair, stretching out in the valley below. I sit rocking on the broad veranda, breathing the sweet air of hillside Tennessee, as we did so long ago. Hummingbirds dive in fast and furious when I hang the nectar pots that draw those airborne jewels. Inside the old home, the same smooth straw matting covers the wide plank pine floors, downstairs and up. The pale green parrots, gold beaked, still swoop across the fading paper on the dining room walls. And there is still no plumbing indoors, in each high-ceilinged bedroom a china pitcher and basin sit atop a washstand, a chamber pot beneath the bed. One bedroom anchors each corner of the fine old house, each claims its own quadrant of the compass, and its own generous view. Valley, meadow, hill, barn.

I slept then, and sleep now, on summer visits, in the pink room. The breeze even in August blows cool off the meadow below, and the light curtains shiver with the soft breath of dawn. I have always loved to rise and swing my bare feet over the edge of the bed onto the cool straw mat and walk to the washstand and pour rainwater—pure, fresh water, pumped the night before from the cistern, waiting all night long in the white porcelain pitcher. Pour the limpid stream into the flowered basin, old china now, its glaze crazed with a fine web of fissures—like the gauze of wrinkles across that familiar face reflected in the cloudy oval wash-stand mirror—my mother's face, but no it's mine grown old.

I plunge my arm into the basin of cool rainwater. It never fails, the liquid kiss brings back the sweet sharp memory of that fugitive summer day. Calls back the taste and touch and sounds of that day, that burning August day, deep in the woods below. My memory, like my sight, like my hearing, sometimes blurs a little now. But the cool water in the flowered bowl pierces the gray shroud of time and decline, and I am young again.

It was a terrible time. Kingdoms had stirred into the war that devoured the young men of Europe, and demanded with rapacious appetite even the youth of Tennessee. Still, the world seemed tranquil up at Yonder Hills. Mountains outlast the strife and grief of man, trees bloom and leaf and fruit, oblivious to war and peace.

My brother had gone as a soldier, leaving his ten-month bride, Birdie, and unborn baby at our home place, Yonder Hills. Bird and I had been dear friends at Grandview Seminary, rooming together in the girls' dormitory. Our teacher Miss Larned used to say, "Grandview is well named. It affords a good view of the Tennessee Valley but also gives those lucky enough to pass this way a Grand View of life and its possibilities." At Grandview I fell in love with books and learning. Upon commencement, I became a teacher there. And Birdie married my brother Walter, and so my friend became my sister.

My first year of school teaching ended. I came to Yonder Hills to care for Bird during the last weeks of her pregnancy—happy to escape the sultry heat of Johnson City, happy to escape my mother's worried supervision of me, her maiden schoolmarm daughter. Happiest to be back at Yonder Hills, my heart's true home, summer home of my childhood.

Birdie, great with child, was tired and awkward. We whiled away late mornings and afternoons on the wide veranda that embraced the house, sipping ice tea in heavy glasses from the corner china cupboard in the dining room. Sun tea steeped on the well platform, garnished with mint from the garden I weeded alone now that she was too stout to stoop and bend. We read aloud to each other. Bird loved poetry and wrote her own verses. We gossiped and remembered our Grandview days. She didn't speak much of Walter, but I sometimes caught her in a moment of soft melancholy, hand cupped on her swell of belly, gazing out into the blue haze of the hills beyond our perch. Birdie was a preacher's daughter, though she wore it lightly, and I knew that she prayed silently for Walter's safe return and for their baby's safe arrival. I knew she kept her Bible marked to the Psalms beside her bed.

Afternoons, she would make her cumbersome way upstairs to nap. Birdie, so called because she was slight and quick, was grown swollen and slow. I followed, to make sure she had a crystal tumbler of water by her bed, that the chamber pot was handy so she would not need to come downstairs to the outhouse. I placed book, embroidery, his latest letter, on her nightstand in case she did not doze. "You're so good to me, Fern," she would sigh from the mound of pillows. I kissed her fragrant cheek, drew the light curtains against the noonday sun, and pulled her tall door closed behind me.

The afternoons were mine to roam the woods behind the house into the steep gully cut by a mountain stream. To ramble in the soft shade of trees rooted to the mountain side: persimmon, tulip tree, and ash. To rest on a carpet of pipsissewa, crowsfoot and partridgeberry beneath the green canopy of mountain laurel and rhododendron.

The waterfall was my destination. Now, I can no longer climb there, can no longer see it except in mind's eye. The falls shot down the rock slope, even in the driest of summers jets of water sparkled and sang. Just below the six-foot drop was a narrow shelf of rock. Water coursed through a deep carved crease and overflowed into a deep pool in the streambed below. As children, we had scrambled down from the rock table to plunge and splash in the crystal pool.

That summer, on my solitary afternoons while Birdie slept, I stripped to chemise and underskirt and swam around and around the little rock bowl. Afterward I stretched out on my stomach on the warm rock, lay there baking my hair and garments dry, staring into the water. Crayfish scuttled across the bottom; water spiders skated the surface.

One afternoon there was a knock at the front door, just as I came down the back stairs into the kitchen, Birdie settled above to rest. We never locked. Our few visitors were all neighbors and friends. I came into the broad, dim entry hall. Looking into the burning August glare beyond the wide screen door, I could only discern a dark shadow, a man's silhouette.

Coming up to the screen I recognized Mr. Edward Holloway, the young Mathematics teacher. He'd come to Grandview in the midyear when old Professor Woodworth fell ill. Mr. Holloway hailed from Cincinnati, how he came to our remote Presbyterian school in the mountains had been a matter of eager speculation among the older girls and the younger teachers like myself. He was tall and fair, and his tenor voice a pleasant addition to our musicales. He became the quiet star of our Literary evenings, held on alternate Fridays, reciting verse as sweetly as he sang.

But what gave me pause, what I remembered on that blazing August afternoon and made me catch my breath in mingled surprise and pleasure, was a cool misted day back in the springtime. He and I had chaperoned the younger children on a picnic. The woods that day were a canvas painted with the bloom of dogwood, redbud, and wild azalea. The ground beneath our feet was blanketed with trailing arbutus. The sweet, waxy pink flower grows so close to the ground you must kneel very close to catch a wisp of its soft, mossy fragrance. A stranger to our southern woods, he knelt and held up a fragile blossom.

"Miss Metzger, what is this?"

I knelt beside him. "Trailing arbutus, Mr. Holloway." Courting couples in our part of the world liked to hunt this flower because it brought you close to each other, close to the ground. My complexion in those days told tales on me. The blush crept from my clavicle to my widow's peak as he gently brushed back my hair and tucked the blossom behind my ear. I almost thought he would lean and kiss me.

Perhaps he would have but for the children rioting nearby. "Who is chaperoning who?" he laughed and pulled me to my feet. Chivalrous, he brushed invisible crumbs of dirt from my skirt and I seemed to feel his touch even through the layers of fabric.

He appeared at the door on that August afternoon and I remembered spring, and hid in the shadow of the hall, betraying blush suffusing my face, giving lie to my casual, courteous welcome.

"Mr. Holloway, how nice to see you. What a pleasant surprise. Won't you come in?"

"Yes, thank you."

I swung the broad screen door open and he stepped in, taller than I had recalled. I led him into the parlor. We sat stiffly there, in the stuffy room, and I regretted the rocking chairs on the airy veranda.

"Miss Metzger, I heard you were here with your sister-in-law. Having the day free, I came to call. I've been tutoring this summer, a family down in Spring City."

"Birdie, Mrs. Metzger, will be sorry to miss your visit. She's resting."

"How is your sister-in-law?"

"Tired, waiting for her time, and waiting for each letter from my brother."

"I imagine it is hard. It is good of you to keep her company."

"I love her like a sister, and I love Yonder Hills. It is a pleasure, truly, to be back here."

"How do you pass your time?"

"Reading—always, everywhere. Afternoons I walk."

"Don't deviate from custom on my account, I should very much like to walk out with you."

"But let me offer you some refreshment. Some iced tea, some lemonade?"

"Not now, thank you but perhaps we might take something with us, in case we develop a thirst on our expedition."

And so I invited him down the dim hallway into the bright kitchen at the back of the house. Led him to the warm heart of our home. The strangeness, the stiffness remained behind in the front parlor. I took a basket from the shelf beside the door, lined it with a soft linen napkin, wrapped a heavy cut glass tumbler in another napkin and placed it in the basket. Leaving him looking out the kitchen window at the sweep of meadow slope behind the house, I went down cellar—always dark and cool there, redolent with the smell of damp and sweet fruit put by. My eyes adjusted to the shadows and I found the store of dandelion wine my brother had made before leaving us for war. I brought a flask upstairs and nested it beside the glass in the basket, added cornbread left from lunch and a crumbling block of cheddar.

"I've packed a little picnic. Shall we go?"

We went, quietly out the back door, careful not to slam and wake Birdie in her room above. Down the steep porch steps, into the burning sun. He stopped and picked two plums as we passed under the gnarled tree. My fingers tingled as the fruit passed from his hand to mine. I dropped the sun warmed plums into the basket, longing to bite into one and taste the sweet nectar.

He stopped at the cistern; pumped the tin cup full of water and handed it to me. I sipped. The still water seemed to bubble against my palate. Gravely he reached for the cup and drank, without wiping the rim my lips had touched. Hanging the cup back in place, he took my hand. We walked, my hand warm in his larger one, under the blazing blue sky, down the sunstruck meadow into the woods.

It was hushed under the leaf-woven awning. The ground cover carpet soaked up the sound of our footfalls. Golden dust motes, the warm, rich fragrance of decaying leaves, rose in the dappled light. We didn't speak. He took the basket and helped me over vines and boughs. I needed no help, sure-footed and familiar with the path but found it keen pleasure to accept his strong hand.

I led him to the falls and up to the ledge. I spread the linen napkin on the stone ledge, making it our table, and handed him a plum, so fresh from the branch it was still sun warm. He bit and red juice ran down his chin like blood. I unwrapped the glass tumbler and blotted his chin with the soft linen napkin, staunching his counterfeit wound, staining the napkin red.

He caught my ministering hand and pulled me close. We embraced and continued the kiss interrupted by our young student chaperones six months earlier. To come together after the interval was sweet reward. After a spell, under a spell, we stopped for breath. I dropped my eyes beneath the warmth of his gaze.

"Here's dandelion wine. My brother's." The amber liquid glowed. I broke the sealing wax around the cork and poured. The everyday cut glass became a chalice I offered. He drank and then, in turn, offered me the golden mead—made from weeds by my brother's alchemy.

He told me he had enlisted. He would not be back at Grandview come autumn. A chill shadow passed over us.

The stone ledge by the falls is narrow but space enough for two to lie upon if close together. We lay together thus. The rock beneath us was warm and we grew warmer.

"We might swim," I whispered.

"Yes," he said, unbuttoning my blouse and gently drawing the ribbon from my camisole as though unwrapping a most precious gift.

We did not bathe in the pool below after all. Rather, we swam together on our rough stone bed into another element, one I had never learned of in Chemistry at Grandview. A new music made me deaf for a time to the purring falls.

The afternoon shadows lengthened and angled and served as our sundial, our signal it was time. I held the glass to rinse it in the falls. Slanting beams of light and water spray, rainbows and prisms, filled the tumbler—reminding me of the recent star dazzle beneath my eyelids as we lay knit together.

The glass slipped through my grasp! Or did I let it go?

It fell into the pool, into a crevice, and wedged there. Laughing, we took it by turns to plunge hand and forearm deep into the narrow rock basin, endeavoring to fish out the glass. My small hand was better sized for rescue but lacked the necessary length of reach. He had the length and strength to reach and grasp, but his hand was too big. The glass was deep in the narrow fissure; held fast. So we left it: a crystal growing into the rock. I did not know as we walked away, leaving the glass in the rock, that he, too, would soon be lost, out of reach, beneath the surface of earth and water.

Though his bones have long since crumbled into dust, I am sure our chalice is still there in the pool. Jammed into the dark crevice, surface tumbled and opalized by water and time, as chips of glass turn to soft edged gems in the sea's inexorable scouring.

I knew heaven on earth, that fugitive day. And plunging my arm into the basin of cool cistern water, brings it back, clear and sharp, my sweet lost day.

Personal Acknowledgements

The author thanks readers at The Bennington Writing Seminars, The Virginia Center for Creative Arts, and the Bethesda Writers Center.

Special gratitude is due to Harold Pskowski, Judy Karasik, Susan Scarf Merrell, Beth Hess, Alice Mattison, Lucy Rosenthal, and Barbara Smith Vargo.

About the Author

Ellen Prentiss Campbell's first collection of stories *Contents Under Pressure* was nominated for the National Book Award. Her debut novel *The Bowl With Gold Seams* received the Indy Excellence Award for Historical Fiction. Short fiction has been recognized by the Pushcart Press. Essays and reviews appear in journals including *The Fiction Writers Review*, where she is a contributing editor, and *The Washington Independent Review of Books*. A graduate of The Bennington Writing Seminars and the Simmons School of Social Work, for many years she practiced psychotherapy. She is at work on a novel. Campbell and her husband live in Washington, D.C. and Manns Choice, Pennsylvania. Connect online at ellencampbell.net

Apprentice
House Press
Loyola University Maryland

Apprentice House is the country's only campus-based, student-staffed book publishing company. Directed by professors and industry professionals, it is a nonprofit activity of the Communication Department at Loyola University Maryland.

Using state-of-the-art technology and an experiential learning model of education, Apprentice House publishes books in untraditional ways. This dual responsibility as publishers and educators creates an unprecedented collaborative environment among faculty and students, while teaching tomorrow's editors, designers, and marketers.

Outside of class, progress on book projects is carried forth by the AH Book Publishing Club, a co-curricular campus organization supported by Loyola University Maryland's Office of Student Activities.

Eclectic and provocative, Apprentice House titles intend to entertain as well as spark dialogue on a variety of topics. Financial contributions to sustain the press's work are welcomed. Contributions are tax deductible to the fullest extent allowed by the IRS.

To learn more about Apprentice House books or to obtain submission guidelines, please visit www.apprenticehouse.com.

Apprentice House
Communication Department
Loyola University Maryland
4501 N. Charles Street
Baltimore, MD 21210
Ph: 410-617-5265
info@apprenticehouse.com
www.apprenticehouse.com

CPSIA information can be obtained
at www.ICGtesting.com
Printed in the USA
BVHW061220210620
581975BV00007B/672

9 781627 202633